Marc ached at ⎯⎯⎯⎯⎯⎯
Ginny and anot ⎯⎯⎯⎯⎯⎯

Was she picturing anoth⎯⎯⎯⎯⎯⎯
her daughter this way? Did she wonder about
finding someone who'd grow to be Hannah's
father eventually? Yes, Marc told himself,
beautiful, wonderful, sweet Ginny would surely
find someone to love again.

So why not me? If Ginny were to decide to
marry again…why not me?

Why not indeed?

Dear Reader,

Holiday greetings from all of us at Silhouette Books to all of you. And along with my best wishes, I wanted to give you a present, so I put together six of the best books ever as your holiday surprise. Emilie Richards starts things off with *Woman Without a Name*. I don't want to give away a single one of the fabulous twists and turns packed into this book, but I *can* say this: You've come to expect incredible emotion, riveting characters and compelling storytelling from this award-winning writer, and this book will not disappoint a single one of your high expectations.

And in keeping with the season, here's the next of our HOLIDAY HONEYMOONS, a miniseries shared with Desire and written by Carole Buck and Merline Lovelace. *A Bride for Saint Nick* is Carole's first Intimate Moments novel, but you'll join me in wishing for many more once you've read this tale of a man who thinks he has no hope of love, only to discover—just in time for Christmas—that a wife and a ready-made family are his for the asking.

As for the rest of the month, what could be better than new books from Sally Tyler Hayes and Anita Meyer, along with the contemporary debuts of historical authors Elizabeth Mayne and Cheryl St.John? So sit back, pick up a book and start to enjoy the holiday season. And don't forget to come back next month for some Happy New Year reading right here at Silhouette Intimate Moments, where the best is always waiting to be unwrapped.

Yours,

Leslie Wainger
Senior Editor and Editorial Coordinator

Please address questions and book requests to:
Silhouette Reader Service
U.S.: 3010 Walden Ave., P.O. Box 1325, Buffalo, NY 14269
Canadian: P.O. Box 609, Fort Erie, Ont. L2A 5X3

SECOND FATHER

SALLY TYLER HAYES

Silhouette®
INTIMATE™MOMENTS®
Published by Silhouette Books
America's Publisher of Contemporary Romance

SILHOUETTE BOOKS

ISBN 0-373-07753-X

SECOND FATHER

Copyright © 1996 by Teresa Hill

Printed in U.S.A.

Books by Sally Tyler Hayes

Silhouette Intimate Moments

SALLY TYLER HAYES

lives in South Carolina with her husband, son and daughter. A former journalist for a South Carolina newspaper, she fondly remembers that her decision to write and explore the frontiers of romance came at about the same time she discovered, in junior high, that she'd never be able to join the crew of the *Starship Enterprise*.

Happy and proud to be a stay-home mom, she is thrilled to be living her lifelong dream of writing romances.

To Melissa Jeglinski,
the kind of editor
most writers
can only dream
of finding.

Prologue

Shots fired.

Officer down.

Delivered in the shorthand of police code, from a police radio rife with static, the message still came through loud and clear.

Chicago police detective Marc Dalton made it to the scene in three minutes flat, because he recognized the voice on the radio. It was his partner, Joseph Reed, Jr.

Until Marc screeched to a stop on the busy Chicago street, bolted from the car and shoved his way to the middle of a crowd of onlookers and worried-looking policemen, he wasn't sure whether his partner was merely the one reporting the incident or the downed officer.

But on the nightmarish drive over, Marc felt the sickness take root in his stomach, then start to grow, moving upward toward the area of his throat, where his intuition always spoke to him. Cops felt things, and they came to trust those feelings.

He wasn't surprised to find Joe lying on the street, a crimson stain spreading across his chest, blood pooling on the asphalt beneath him.

Marc dropped to his knees beside his partner. A fellow officer from another precinct was holding a cloth against the wound in Joe's chest. The officer's gaze met Marc's for a second, then he shook his head and looked away.

Swallowing hard, Marc bent over his partner and called to him. Joe moaned, then winced as he turned toward Marc's voice.

Finally Joe roused enough to recognize him. "Marc?"

"I'm here, buddy."

"So many things... to tell you," he said with great effort.

"Take it easy, Joe. The ambulance is right behind me."

Joe shook his head weakly. "No time..." he whispered. "Aw, jeez... what a stupid-ass thing to do.... Marc?"

"I'm here."

"Ginny?"

"What about Ginny?" Marc asked, referring to Joe's wife.

"Take care of her?"

Marc choked on the words. "I will."

"Promise?"

"Swear to God, Joey, I will."

"Tell her... I'm sorry."

And then Joseph Reed, Jr., was gone.

In a daze, sometime later, Marc looked around and caught the glare of a TV crew's lights on the perimeter of the scene, and he knew he had to begin fulfilling the promise he'd made to Joe.

Marc made his way to a small two-story house to the west of the city. He knocked on the door and watched as the pretty young woman who answered it recoiled in horror at the look on his face and the bloodstains on his shirt.

She looked around frantically for a man who would never come home to her again. Marc took her into his arms as she went from denial to disbelief to bitter tears with lightning speed.

And he held on to her. For the first time, he held Ginny Reed in his arms, as he'd so often longed to do.

But a quiet refrain reverberated inside his head.

Aw, Ginny, not like this.

Chapter 1

Chapter 1

One year later...

"Detective, let's go over it one more time," said Ronald Gerard, a gruff, worn-looking eighteen-year veteran of the Chicago Police Department.

Marc, seated in a utilitarian plastic chair at a bare table in a small, windowless room at the downtown police headquarters, shifted to face the officer, who'd circled behind his back and now stood just off his left shoulder.

Marc knew the routine. He'd questioned hundreds of suspects in similar rooms, using similar tactics. But *he'd* never been questioned before.

He worked hard to show no emotion at the announcement that they would be going over things *one more time*. That meant they would go over it again and again until these two detectives gave up, found some inconsistencies in his statement or made him so mad he'd say something he shouldn't.

And if either of these two men from internal affairs knew how close Marc was to blowing his cool, they'd hound him even harder. Marc couldn't afford to give them that kind of advantage.

Gerard picked up with Marc's story. "On the morning Detective Reed was shot, the two of you were working a homicide."

"Yes," Marc said.

"And you had plans for that morning?"

"We planned to locate the victim's sister."

"And the sister was where?"

"In an apartment complex in Richmond Hills, we thought."

"Nowhere near downtown?"

"No."

"And Detective Reed failed to show up at the station that morning?"

"Yes."

"And what was his explanation when he called you about that?"

Marc worked hard at saying it without any emotion, and damned Joe Reed as he did. "He said he had an errand to run."

"An errand that involved some sort of official police business?"

"I don't know."

"You don't know?" Gerard asked, his voice full of innuendo.

Marc was seething. He looked to his left, to a detective named O'Connor, a tall, slender, quiet man Marc believed to be a good friend of Joe's father. Joe Reed, Sr., was a well-respected thirty-year veteran of the police force, a man not without clout. O'Connor remained stoic and silent. Apparently Marc and Joe were on their own here.

"I didn't ask," Marc finally answered.

Gerard nodded, satisfied with making what he would of that. "Now, you and Detective Reed were partners for how long?"

"Six years."

"And you knew him well?"

Marc hesitated. Until the last few months before the shooting, he would have said he knew Joe Reed, Jr., better than anyone. Joe had been Marc's first and only partner, and the closest thing Marc Dalton had to family.

"Detective?"

Marc was simmering. "Yes, I knew him well."

"And was Detective Reed in the habit of running personal errands during his shifts?"

Again Marc hesitated. In those last few months of his life, Joe had developed some nasty habits Marc didn't want to get into here. Still, there could have been any number of explanations for that—ones that had nothing to do with what Gerard was insinuating.

"Joe Reed was one hell of a cop," Marc said, knowing he'd blown it right then and there.

The man questioning him closed in for the kill. "So what was he doing in front of that apartment building that day? How did he happen to be right there when the shooting started? Exactly how did he end up dead?"

"I don't know," Marc said. "You tell me."

"He was dirty."

O'Connor chose that moment to enter the fray. "We don't know that, Gerard. We don't know much of anything right now, especially why a man with ten years' service and a spotless record died nearly a year ago."

"He wasn't a dirty cop," Marc said, wishing whatever nagging doubts he had on that very subject didn't keep him awake at night.

"Then we need to prove that, if that is indeed the truth," O'Connor said. "We need to find out exactly why Joe Reed died."

Marc glanced over at Gerard. He knew the man wasn't here to prove Joe Reed's innocence. Marc understood the political power play he'd been thrown into. Either Joe's father or his father's friends had managed to get O'Connor, who was sympathetic to Joe's case, this job of investigating Joe's death. Ronald Gerard, who thought Joe had been the scum of the earth, was here to even things out.

"Does the family know anything about this investigation?" Marc turned to O'Connor for the answer.

"No," O'Connor replied, "but we're going to have to move fast, before word gets out. And we need your help. We need to know what you know, Detective. Will you help us clear this thing up before it gets all blown out of proportion?"

Marc looked at O'Connor, whom he trusted, and Gerard, whom he did not, and decided to talk a little longer. "What do you want to know?"

"You really don't know what Joe was doing in front of that apartment building the day he was shot?" O'Connor asked.

"No." It was the truth. And much as Marc hated to admit it, it hurt.

"There's nothing about the homicide you two were investigating at the time that would have taken him to that area?"

"No."

"There isn't anyone caught up in this police corruption scandal that's linked to Joe in any way?"

"No." Marc saw all too clearly where this line of questioning was leading, and it made him sick. His partner hadn't been killed by just anybody. Joe Reed had been shot by a cop—a dirty cop, one William Welsh Morris, who was headed for trial soon on first-degree-murder charges.

Marc sat back in his chair. "Something's convinced you that you haven't caught everyone involved in this scandal yet."

"We're not sure," Gerard said.

"And we need your help, Detective," O'Connor added.

"I've answered your questions."

"Sorry," O'Connor said. "I'm afraid we're going to need more from you than that."

Ginny Reed made it through the service just fine, considering that the last time she'd entered this church had been the day she'd buried her husband—one full year ago this month. Through sheer force of will, she calmly endured the small reception at her own home following the baptism of her baby daughter, born eight and a half months after Joe had been killed.

Surrounded by still-grieving relatives, their faces somber, their tones hushed, their tears flowing freely at times, Ginny felt the cracks spreading through the foundation of her hard-won composure. As at the funeral, all eyes were on her. As she had then, she held her head high, sank her teeth into her bottom lip when necessary and kept her tears at bay. She wasn't a woman given to public displays of emotion, and she'd never quite gotten used to the full-blown crush of Joe's big extended family. They overwhelmed her at times, especially now that Joe wasn't here to act as a buffer.

"Excuse me," she said to her mother-in-law, who had been married to Joseph Reed, Sr., for nearly half a century, "I think I hear Hannah fussing."

"I'll get her, dear," said the older woman. Mama Reed was nicely rounded, and kind-hearted, but she had a backbone of steel. A year after Joe's death, she still dressed in black from head to toe as a sign of respect for her son.

"No, I'll get the baby. It's almost feeding time," insisted Ginny, who'd chosen a deep plum sweater and skirt for the occasion, not wanting to be in mourning clothes in the photographs from her daughter's baptism.

Surely someday Joe's mother would come to understand that Hannah's baptism wasn't a time for mourning. Someday Ginny wanted to look back on this day and remember the joy she'd found in having a daughter, rather than the pain of losing her husband just before they finally realized their dream of having a family.

Ginny had kept to herself as much as possible during the past year by working at the accounting firm she'd been with since graduating from the nearby community college and awaiting the birth of her baby. In the next few months, she planned to start working part-time from home for the same accounting firm, thanks to the computer and modem she would set up in the spare bedroom. With that income and Joe's life insurance, she and Hannah were going to be fine. If they were careful, Ginny might not have to go back to work full-time until Hannah was in school.

Glancing up, Ginny saw one of Joe's aunt's, tears glistening in the woman's eyes, approaching. It was time to escape, if she could.

Wordlessly, careful to keep from making eye contact with Grandma and Grandpa Reed, Joe's father, his two brothers, his cousins and assorted other members of the Reed clan, Ginny slipped through the crowd. She went down the hall, up the stairs and into the back bedroom, which she and Joe had planned to paint a sunny yellow. But that had been more than ten years ago, when they first planned to start a family. They had never dreamed it would take so long to have a baby.

In the white crib in the corner near the window, surrounded by the faint blue clouds on the ceiling and a menagerie of stuffed animals, lay Miss Hannah Reed in a pink-and-white polka-dot sleeper.

Hannah slept with her chest and arms flush against the mattress, her knees drawn up under her and her little bottom sticking up in the air. The side of her face was pressed against the mattress, and one hand was in a fist, the knuckles hunched against lips that smacked and sucked frantically against them.

One of the greatest frustrations of Hannah's young life was the fact that she couldn't get her whole fist into her greedy little mouth. Ginny couldn't help but smile, even if her happiness was bittersweet.

"Oh, Hannah..." She reached into the crib and rested her hand against the baby, feeling the reassuring rise and fall of Hannah's back with every breath the infant took.

Losing Joe had shown Ginny that, in an instant, everything could change. And, at times, left her with the urge to just stand here and watch Hannah breathe.

Ginny walked to the window and looked outside. She glanced at her watch, calculated that if she could make it through the next twenty minutes or so—perhaps by hiding out in this room—people would start leaving. She could simply go out, say goodbye and send them all on their way. The house would be hers and Hannah's once again, with no anxious eyes watching her every move, no one taking the measure of her grief for Joe and finding it lacking.

Just because Ginny didn't cry in public, that didn't mean she wasn't grieving. Just because she could smile and laugh at her wondrous baby girl, that didn't mean she'd forgotten about losing Joe.

Surely, in time, Joe's family would come to understand.

Ginny sighed and turned back toward the crib. That telltale tingling and heaviness in her breasts told her Hannah was about to wake up and demand her dinner. It was funny how in tune mother and daughter could be. Ginny could be in the next room, on the first floor, even, and still know moments before Hannah was ready to awaken and start howling to be fed.

Grabbing the receiving blanket that was draped across the back of the rocker, Ginny went back to the crib and watched her daughter. Hannah started bouncing, up on her knees, then down again, her bottom rocking back and forth in the air as she struggled to keep from waking.

When the rocking motion failed to soothe her, Hannah gave it up and attacked her knuckles once again. When that didn't work, she stretched, her face scrunched up in a grimace at the effort that took. The baby slipped over onto her side and finally opened her startlingly blue eyes. She blinked once, then again, then started to wail, the hunger hitting her the instant she awakened.

"Shhh..." Ginny reached for her. "You'll have the whole houseful of people in here in a minute, and Mama doesn't need that right now."

She gave Hannah a little kiss, then settled them both in the rocker. Quickly, efficiently, Ginny pulled up her sweater, flicked open her bra with one hand and took Hannah to her breast. The baby knew just what she wanted, sucking vigorously, sometimes faster than she could swallow. Ginny grabbed a fresh cloth diaper and wiped her daughter's chin and her cheek before both of them were soaked in the milk that missed Hannah's mouth.

Hannah latched on to Ginny's ring finger with her right hand and held on tight. That meant Ginny had better not try to get away, because Hannah wasn't done yet.

Ginny sat back and closed her eyes, the fresh new-baby smell and the sweet scent of the milk settling over her. Hannah's warmth and her weight soaked into her. Contentment, short-lived and so odd in the face of this much unhappiness, surrounded her.

And then, tired, her defenses all used up, Ginny started to cry.

Chapter 2

Marc drove around for nearly an hour, missed the baptism altogether, but swung by the house for the reception. The house was still surrounded by cars—no fewer than three of them police vehicles—when Marc arrived, two hours late. He glanced at the place, a long, narrow two-story brick home, on a block of two-story brick homes. They had tiny front yards, cracked sidewalks and porches full of wicker chairs and blooming baskets of hanging plants.

He'd been here many times, had in fact considered it almost a second home in the years he was partnered with Joe. And he'd never been more torn about whether to make his way inside.

Too many questions, too many doubts and fears, filled his head.

He didn't have any idea what to do now. How could he possibly take on this job he'd been asked to do?

Yet he had questions of his own about Joe's death. He wanted answers, for himself, for Joe, and for Joe's family.

Still, could he betray his partner and the Reed clan this way? Because that was how he saw it—as a betrayal.

Unerringly his thoughts turned from Joe to Ginny. He'd suffered through many days and nights, thinking about Ginny Reed. His guilt was enormous, and yet he couldn't help but think of her.

No woman should have to live through what Ginny had faced in the past year—burying her husband, finding out she was finally pregnant with the child they'd wanted for so long, going through that pregnancy alone, and now raising that child by herself.

How would sweet, gentle Ginny handle that? And what business of his was it, anyway? He was next to nothing to Ginny Reed now, nothing but her dead husband's ex-partner.

Marc had no idea what he was going to do about the myriad of feelings he had for Joe's widow. But he made one simple decision. He was going inside this house tonight. Maybe, somewhere in there, he would find some answers.

Marc's knock was answered by Joe's cousin Antonio, a beefy, quick-tempered rookie cop. He shook the kid's hand, then shook hands with a half dozen other men in the room, all of whom he knew by name. Joe's dad seemed to have aged ten years in the twelve months since Joe's death and his own heart attack. Mr. Reed patted Marc on the back and thanked him for coming.

Ben Reed, a shorter, slightly older version of Joe, waved from his spot on the living room sofa. Joe's other brother, Jimmy, came over to shake Marc's hand.

The room was crowded to the point of overflowing, and ninety percent of the people here were either named Reed or related by blood to someone who was.

Marc hadn't seen the entire clan together like this since Joe's funeral. It was hard to see them all together and not look around, expecting Joe to pop out of the crowd at any moment. From the somber air of the people in the room, Marc realized the situation must be harder on Joe's family.

Someone offered Marc cake, someone else tried to tempt him with punch and finally a sandwich, which he accepted to give himself something to do with his hands. Then he settled into a corner and searched the room for Ginny and the baby. Finding no sign of either of them, he finally asked Joe's mother, a second-generation Italian known all over the neighborhood for her nosiness and her cooking. When she directed him upstairs, to the back bedroom, Marc hesitated.

"Go ahead," Mama Reed told him. "Ginny spends too much time in this house all alone with the baby. Get her to come back here with the rest of us."

Marc didn't like the sound of Ginny and the baby being alone so often, and once again he questioned the reason he'd stayed away from here for most of the past year.

Guilt was part of it, but what of the rest? He couldn't begin to understand it—except that Ginny Reed had always made him feel things he had no right to feel, not before her husband's death and certainly not afterward.

Marc glanced back and saw that Mama Reed was still watching him. Taking a deep breath, squaring his shoulders, swallowing the lump in his throat, he climbed the stairs and tapped lightly on the door. At Ginny's quiet-spoken invitation, he went inside.

She was sitting in the corner, in the rocker, the baby lying across her lap in the dimly lit room. He got a quick impression of hazy white clouds along the ceiling, dozens of pairs of eyes from the miniature zoo of stuffed animals, all watching him intently. And the baby, wrapped in pink-and-white polka dots, was resting quietly against her mother.

Ginny. Even after all these years, the sight of her still had the power to take him completely by surprise. It was like turning around and walking into a wall. She absolutely took his breath away.

She looked a little tired, her complexion pale against the dark knit of her sweater. Her honey-blond hair was loose, hanging down around her shoulders in rings of curls. Her eyes were wet, her lashes spiked together with tears, and her teeth were sunk into her bottom lip. She had one of her hands around the baby. A finger of her other hand was enclosed in one tiny baby hand. Her tears spilled over from her eyelids, making a slow, solemn trail down her cheek.

"I'm sorry," Marc said. "I can come back...."

"No." As she tried to avert her face so that he wouldn't see, he noticed another tear falling down her cheek.

Marc watched as Ginny tried to pull her finger out of the baby's fist, but Hannah gave a rumbling sound of protest and held on fast. Before he could question the wisdom of getting that close—of touching Joe's baby and wiping away the tears of Joe's wife—Marc was beside them, propelled by an emotion he simply could not understand.

"Insistent little thing, isn't she?" He knelt in front of Ginny and the baby.

Ginny gave him a weak smile. "Hannah's very protective of her dinner."

Marc didn't understand at first. Then, finally, it dawned on him, when he saw only the baby's cheek and one tiny ear visible, the rest hidden beneath Ginny's sweater. She was nursing the baby, and now he was sure he was intruding. "I'll come back. Really."

"It's fine," Ginny insisted, her tears slowing now. "You're the third person who's interrupted us. Actually, it might help if you'd stay. You could guard the door."

"Sure," he said, oddly drawn to the sight of mother and child this way, yet uneasy at the same time. He knew women nursed babies all the time, in all sorts of places. But it seemed like such an intimate thing.

Ginny tried again to get one hand free. Hannah growled in protest.

Marc laughed some of the tension away. "Three and a half months and you've already got a female who knows how to get her way."

Ginny gave him a weak smile, and then he couldn't help it—he put his hand on the side of her face.

"It's all right," he said when she stiffened and nearly pulled away. With the pads of his thumbs, he wiped her tears, brushed away the ones that had fallen onto the baby's cheek, as well. Then he stood and backed up three steps.

Ginny's face flamed, and she averted her eyes. "Thank you," she said.

Not knowing what to do next, he took his post by the door, all the while telling himself he shouldn't have touched her. He had no right to touch her.

But the scene was breaking his heart. She deserved so much better than to be in this room, alone with her baby and her tears, with no one to brush them away.

"I'm glad you came today," Ginny said finally.

"Sorry I missed the ceremony at the church. Something came up at work."

"I know how that goes."

He was sure she did. Joe had been a cop the entire time they were married. "It must have been difficult for you, being back in the church today."

She nodded.

"I wish... Aw, hell, Ginny, I know everything has to be difficult for you now, so it's no use telling you I'm sorry being in that church again was so hard. Truth is, I don't know what to say except that it's all so damned unfair. And I shouldn't have stayed away so long."

She shook her head. "It's all right. Nobody knows what to say, and I really don't expect anyone to be able to make sense out of something I can't even begin to understand myself. I'm just glad you're here now."

"I'd do anything I could to make this easier for you."

She looked him right in the eye then. "Do you mean that?"

"Yes."

She began to tell him something, but Hannah chose that moment to start squirming. Her face popped out from beneath her mother's sweater and she turned to Marc and cooed. She had enormous dark eyes, big, puffy cheeks, a button nose and rosebud lips. She blinked at him twice, held out one hand to him and cooed again.

"Oh, man, what a heartbreaker."

"And a flirt. I think she wants you to hold her. Do you mind?"

Marc hesitated. He was an only child and didn't know a thing about babies—except that Hannah Reed was just about the prettiest little thing he'd ever seen.

"She won't break," Ginny reassured him.

"You're sure?"

"Jimmy and Barbara's little boy, Benjie, got her out of her car seat and carried her around the house the other day before anyone noticed."

"You're kidding? That kid's what—four?"

"Three."

Marc felt a little weak in the knees.

"She's sturdy. I promise."

"Well, I guess if Benjie can handle her, I can, too." He walked over to the rocker and let her put Hannah into his arms. He noticed the baby's scent first, baby powder and something else he couldn't identify, a freshness, a newness. And her skin was soft. He touched her cheek again, and was reminded of wiping away Ginny's tears.

Hannah would not be ignored. She purred like a kitten and grinned at him. She kept batting her nearly nonexistent eyelashes at him, as well, while her eyes, almost a violet color, stared intently at him. Her hair was a deep, dark blonde, like her mother's, but something about the eyes reminded him of Joe.

He felt a powerful sadness wash over him, like a wave with the power to knock him to his knees. Joe would never have the chance to hold her this way. He'd never smell this wonderful baby scent or feel the softness of her cheek.

"Don't do that," Ginny said. "Please, don't."

"Do what?"

"Think about Joe. Not now."

"I'm sorry."

"It's just that so many people look at her and think of him. I'm afraid she's going to think the sight of her is enough to make the whole world dissolve into tears."

"I didn't even realize..."

"I just want her to know what it is to be happy. I want her surrounded by laughter and smiles and joy and everything good about the world. Can you understand that?''

"Of course." From the way she explained it, he could tell not everyone understood. "The Reed clan is getting to you?"

Ginny sighed. "Oh, Marc. Nobody else seems to realize that. I know she looks like Joe. I look into her eyes, and it's like looking into his. And I do miss him. But I've cried for months now, and I just can't cry anymore. I know—I was crying when you came in, but not about losing Joe, not exactly, anyway."

"Do you want to tell me about it?"

"Could I?"

"Of course."

Hannah chose that moment to latch on to Marc's right ear and pull for all she was worth.

"Hey, watch it, squirt." He carefully freed his ear, then hung on to her surprisingly strong, yet tiny, hand.

The baby sighed and batted her lashes.

"She likes to be the center of attention," Ginny explained.

"Typical," he said, amazed. "And she knows how to flirt and how to get what she wants. This is scary. She's not even four months old. How can she know all these things already?"

"She's very smart."

"She's a woman already.

"I think she's my reward—that God is trying to even the score in some way, to make up for Joe being gone. She's just incredible. She's going to get me through this."

Marc tucked the baby firmly against him and held on tight, then risked holding out his other hand and offering it to Ginny. She latched on to it, her touch tentative at first, then stronger as her hand clasped his.

"You're going to come through this just fine. I know you will."

She turned all glassy-eyed on him for a second, then got herself under control. "I am so glad you came today."

"Me too."

"You meant it earlier, when you said you'd do anything you could to help us?"

"Absolutely."

"There are some things I want to ask you," she said, then stopped when someone tapped on the door.

"Ginny?" It was Joe's brother Ben. "You okay in there?"

"Fine. We'll be out in a minute."

She waited until she heard his footsteps moving away from the door.

"So," Ginny said, looking him in the eye and trying to summon a smile, "were all of them still there when you came in? Hasn't anyone made a move for the door?"

He thought back to the moment he'd entered the crowded room. "How many people were there when you came upstairs?"

"Twenty-five or so."

"I'm afraid you picked up a few since then."

"They won't give the two of us a minute's peace while they're here," she said. "Do you think you could come by later? Hannah goes to bed about eight-thirty. We could talk then."

"Sure."

Marc waited for her to explain, but she didn't say anything else. He handed her the baby, smoothed Hannah's hair, then leaned over and kissed her cheek.

"She's a beauty," he said. *Just like her mother.* "I'll see you two later."

They made their way downstairs together. He stepped aside while she made her way back into the crush of people in the living room. Then Marc slipped out the kitchen door. He wondered what she wanted to talk to him about, wondered whether Ginny knew anything about the things set in motion already by the police department. He hoped she didn't.

Her husband had been painted as a fallen hero and given a hero's burial. Her face had become well-known around town as the media played up the story for all it was worth—particularly the part about the child Joe hadn't lived to see.

It was up to Marc to protect her and Hannah now, as Joe couldn't. And he would protect Joe's memory, as well. If only he could figure out how to go about doing that.

Shortly after seven, Ginny finally closed the door on Jimmy and his wife, Barbara, and Antonio and Sharon, his bride-to-be—as she'd come to be known within the family circle, because the poor girl seemed destined to be his fiancée for the rest of her life. Antonio showed no interest in actually marrying her. The four of them were the last to leave the baptism.

Exhausted from the emotional strain of the day, Ginny sat down on the floor of the sun room, which also served as Hannah's playroom. In the middle of the toy-covered floor, on a blanket, lay Hannah on her stomach. She was alternately batting at a ball, chewing on a rattle and eyeing the potted plant in the corner.

For now, all she could do was inch forward and backward on her belly, but soon Hannah would have her way with anything that caught her eye and fell within her reach. Ginny could just see herself now, begging Hannah to be nice to the pretty plant in the corner or rescuing the delicate china figurines on the coffee table when Hannah became old enough to stand and cruise around the table.

Ten long years of struggling to have a baby, and Ginny had truly no idea what it would be like to actually have one. She had just known that for the longest time she'd wanted a baby more than anything, and for some reason she couldn't understand, God had not seen fit to give her one.

She laughed at the irony of it—her prayers answered, her precious baby here, babbling and slobbering over a toy in front of her, her husband gone forever.

Ginny had her heart's desire now, her Hannah, but everything else had changed. She missed Joe, and didn't think that particular ache would ever get better. Sometimes the mixture of love and anger and longing came down upon her, so heavily its weight nearly crushed her.

She missed the early years with her husband, when she'd thought Joe and his big, loud, loving family were going to make all her dreams come true. Ginny Alexander, the girl who'd lost her parents when she was ten, then found herself being raised by a sometimes sour and stuffy fifty-year-old maiden aunt, had wanted a family just like Joe's. She'd coveted his two brothers and one sister, the cousins, the eccentric aunts and boisterous uncles, the grandparents—everything. The raucous dinners, the constant parade of people in and out, the roar of the children running from room to room. Ginny had wanted all of that. And once, not so long ago, she had loved Joe.

How had all that slipped through her fingers? She just wished she could go back to the beginning with Joe and make everything right. And this time she'd find a way to hang on to it all.

Hannah chose that moment to make a low rumbling sound in her throat, something reminiscent of a lion cub's roar, then threw the rattle to the carpet beneath her. She jibber-jabbered to herself for a minute, then picked up a powder puff lying next to her seat. Hannah loved the feel of the powder puff against her skin, but she had a bad habit of trying to eat that, too.

"Oh, no, you don't, little girl." Ginny snatched it away from her.

Hannah pouted, her lips falling into a frown, her eyes tearing up in seconds. It was a well-practiced routine. Manipulation was Hannah's forte. Ginny stroked the baby's cheek with the powder puff. Hannah made a grab for it and missed, pouted for another moment, then tried to eat her mama's fingers.

Ginny couldn't help but smile. She lay down on her back on the floor beside her daughter. Hannah leaned over and touched her mother's face, as if she sensed the sadness inside Ginny and wanted to do her best to make it better.

"You do, Hannah banana," Ginny whispered, stroking the baby's soft, blond hair. "You always know just how to make Mama feel better."

The doorbell rang not fifteen minutes later. Ginny stared at the clock, then at the messy house, and thought about trying to ignore the summons. But it was probably one of the Reeds, and if she didn't answer the door, they'd call, and call, and call. If that produced no response, they'd send a patrol car over to check the house.

Someday, maybe in the next decade, they'd understand that she wasn't nearly as fragile as they believed.

The doorbell rang again. Hannah, who wasn't at all sleepy, was looking all around the room, trying to figure out where the pretty sound came from.

Ginny made her way to the entryway and looked through the peephole. Surprised and happy at finding Marc standing there, she threw open the door. "You're early. I was afraid Antonio and his bride-to-be were back."

"You don't like Antonio?"

"More that I don't care for the bride-to-be. She wants babies, lots of babies, and she decided to show off her parenting skills on poor Hannah too soon after feeding time. When I wasn't looking, she bounced Hannah so hard my poor little girl threw up."

"All over the bride-to-be?"

Ginny smiled. She had forgotten that part. "Yes. I'm not sure if Antonio's going to be a father anytime soon, after hearing the words that came out of that sweet girl's mouth."

Marc handed two brown bags to her. "Mama Reed was worried. She said you're not eating properly and that you didn't take a bite all afternoon."

Ginny got a whiff of what she prayed was chicken enchiladas from the Mexican restaurant down the street. Her stomach growled, even as she wondered whether she could eat what was in the bags without upsetting Hannah. Spicy foods didn't mix well with breast-feeding.

"I see Mama Reed was right," Marc said.

"This time, she was."

"I called the restaurant the minute I saw the last two cars leave."

"Thank you," she said, not sure she liked the idea of Marc or anyone else watching her house.

"You looked all done in this afternoon. I thought Hannah and I could get better acquainted for a while, so you can eat and then....I don't know. What do new mothers long to do when they get a break from mothering?''

"A bath," Ginny said, before she thought the idea through. Then she found herself feeling a little uncomfortable at the idea of taking off all her clothes and soaking in the tub while Marc was downstairs.

But Marc was practically family, she argued with herself. There was no need to feel uneasy.

"A bath?" Clearly he didn't understand the appeal.

"It's a woman thing. Maybe Hannah will explain it to you." Ginny took the bag from him, not knowing which she wanted more—food or the blessed peace and quiet of her own tub.

"Where is Hannah?"

"In the sun room. Are you hungry? Do you want to eat now?"

"I already ate at the party." He walked past her toward the sun room.

"This is all for me? The bag weighs a ton."

"Mama Reed said to feed you right for a change, and I wasn't sure what you'd like. Any special instructions for handling Hannah?"

"Don't let her eat the plant in the corner."

Marc frowned. "You're joking, right?"

Ginny shook her head. "The other day, I found her clawing at the basket it's sitting in and growling. And watch yourself. She pulled my hair this evening after you left."

"Surely I can hold my own against an infant."

"You're about to find out."

Ginny waited, watching him make his way through the living room to the sun room, where Hannah was playing. He scooped the baby up off the floor and kissed her on the nose. Hannah cooed and batted at his cheek with one tiny hand.

Deep inside Ginny, something twisted and strained against itself. Something ached, to the point where she was near to tears at the sight of her daughter fussing over this man, then lovingly laying her head against his chest and snuggling against him.

Why couldn't it have been Joe?

Ginny turned abruptly, blinking back her tears, and headed up the stairs.

Why did Joe have to die? she wondered again.

Maybe Marc knew. Or could find out. Maybe he would explain to her what no one else in the Reed family would.

Chapter 3

Miss Hannah Reed was a charmer, even if she was a whimpering, simpering, manipulative, demanding female. Marc got down on the floor with her and pulled out all her toys from the basket in the corner. Then, as he watched, she discarded each one and looked as if she expected him to magically produce more.

"Just like a woman, Hannah, never satisfied."

She blinked, showing off her baby blues.

"I know. I know," he reassured her. "You're a doll, but beauty isn't everything, little girl."

Hannah blew out air against half-closed lips, which fluttered against one another, making a rather rude sound.

"Well, I guess you told me, didn't you?"

Marc would never have believed a kid who couldn't talk could express herself so well. He would have sworn that inside that pretty little head of hers was a brain that missed nothing. Lord, if Hannah was like this now, what should she be like at five? Or fifteen?

"You're going to be a handful," he told her, all of a sudden missing Joe more than ever.

He and Joe had been neighbors growing up, although they hadn't had much to do with one another in the early years. Joe had been five years older than Marc, who hung out with one of Joe's cousins from time to time. That was how Marc had come to know the Reed clan. They were mostly cops, fire fighters and military men—service was in their blood—and their wives stayed home and had babies. Lots of babies. No one ever moved too far away, and around the holidays the Reed house was an absolute zoo.

Marc's father had been killed in the early years of the Vietnam War. He and his mother, a teenage war bride, lived with his grandmother for years. Then his mother had remarried and moved away, leaving Marc behind with his grandmother.

He couldn't say he'd led an unhappy life. On the job, on the streets, he'd seen kids who had it much worse than he ever had. But when he saw the Reeds, he was always reminded of how much he'd missed.

Being partnered with Joe right out of the police academy and being pulled into the Reed clan as a surrogate member of the family had been wonderful, until he reached the point where he couldn't keep his thoughts off Ginny.

Ginny, who was upstairs soaking in the bathtub right now. He jerked around, feeling like a Peeping Tom, when all he'd done was picture her like that in his mind.

Hannah, tired of being ignored, started fussing and tugging on his hair. Marc picked her up, held her close and felt even lonelier than ever.

Just as Marc had never seen his father, Hannah would never see hers.

"I'm so sorry, baby girl," he said, knowing what she would go through in later years.

Hannah must have been tired, because she put her head against his chest and started sucking at the sides of her fingers. Marc had his hand against her back, making little circles there against the fabric of her pink sleeper, putting his nose against her hair and inhaling that intoxicatingly sweet baby smell.

The pressure began building in his head, behind his eyes. He wasn't ashamed to admit that he'd shed tears of his own the day he came to this house and held Ginny in his arms after telling her Joe had died. He could easily have shed some more right now, over Joe's daughter.

But he remembered what Ginny had told him. Little Hannah should know more than tears. Marc forced a smile onto his face. He stood with Hannah in his arms and walked to the CD player in the corner, selecting something at random. The room filled with soft, mournful music, a love song with a lot of sax and a heavy beat. Marc started to hum and to sway in time to the music.

"May I have this dance, young lady?"

Hannah gurgled happily. Shuffling his feet and swaying in rhythm with the song, with Hannah pressed close against his aching heart, Marc felt a little better.

Marc was still dancing with Hannah when Ginny came back down. Marc looked up and saw her standing in the doorway. She was covered from head to toe in a big pink bathrobelike thing of heavy terry cloth, with buttons from head to toe. Her cheeks were flushed, and her hair was piled on top of her head, the tendrils damp and curling at the nape of her neck. He thought he could smell some kind of perfumed soap, or maybe some lotion. Then he could no longer keep from his mind the vision of her lying in the tub, covered with bubbles, the outline of her body visible just below the surface of the water.

In the midst of a note, he stopped humming, stopped shuffling his feet, almost stopped breathing. This was going to be more difficult than he realized. Being with Ginny, even now, was going to require all his hard-won self-control.

She was watching him so intently now, in a way that made him all too aware of the fact that they were alone in the house, late at night.

He was her husband's friend, he reminded himself sternly, and her husband was dead. What kind of a man stood in his friend's home and let these kinds of thoughts about his friend's widow run through his head?

Marc had no answers.

Finally Ginny asked, "Is she actually asleep?"

"I think so, but I had her to sleep a few minutes ago, too. She woke up the minute I tried to put her down."

"She napped later than usual, so she probably wasn't ready then."

Ginny stayed in the doorway. Marc stayed where he was, a good ten feet away. That had seemed safe enough at first. Now he was starting to wonder.

"Why don't you try putting her down upstairs, in her crib, and I'll warm up some of the food for us. You can stay, can't you? And help me eat some of it?"

If he didn't choke on it, he thought he might manage. Still, not wanting to dwell on that challenge, he simply nodded and headed for the stairs.

"Put her down on her side," Ginny called softly to him. "And rub her back for a minute. She likes that."

Marc did as he was told. Then he stood in the dark, quiet nursery and listened to Hannah—not quite awake and not quite asleep—sucking furiously against her little fist.

He felt the past closing in on him, felt memories flooding back that he could no longer keep at bay. He couldn't help but recall the first time he'd seen Ginny. She'd grown up nearby, as well, attended the same schools he had, and she and Marc had always been friends. When Marc was fifteen, his grandmother's heart had given out. He'd finally gotten to live with his mother and her new family, although he'd never felt as if he belonged there. After three years of trying to make that arrangement work, he'd moved back to Chicago and the neighborhood that he would always consider his home. Ginny had been eighteen, as well, and she was about to marry Joe Reed.

Marc had always liked Joe, admired him, even. And Marc wasn't the kind of man to hit on a married woman, especially a woman who belonged to a friend of his. But he just couldn't get Ginny out of his mind.

He remembered a conversation they had had one warm spring night, in the midst of one of Joe and Ginny's prewedding parties. Marc and Ginny had ended up on the patio in an attempt to escape from the noise and the crowds inside the Reed house. They had talked about family. Marc knew Ginny wanted a big family as much as he did. He thought sometimes she might have married Joe as much for his family as for the man himself. Or maybe that was wishful thinking on his part.

At the time, marriage hadn't been something that weighed heavily on Marc's mind. He'd gone from job to job for a couple of years, searching for something that felt right to him. Then he'd been accepted into the police academy, and later partnered with Joe, and nearly everything had seemed right for a while.

The older he got, the more women he dated, the more he'd thought of Ginny. Since he was Joe's partner, it hadn't been unusual for Marc to be invited to the house. As a longtime family friend, he'd often found himself at Mama Reed's home, as well, along with the rest of the clan.

Ginny Reed had become the standard against which he measured every other woman he met, and he'd never found one he admired more than her, never found one he wanted as much as he'd grown to want her.

He couldn't have said exactly why she'd become so important to him, why her image, her voice, the feel of her hand in his or a light kiss of his lips against her cheek stayed so firmly implanted in some corner of his mind, no matter how hard he tried to pry those memories out.

Ginny was a pretty woman, although she didn't have the face or the figure that graced magazine covers or the kind of presence that had men's heads turning. She was a quiet, peaceful, restful person. She was kind, sweet, generous—so unlike most of the women he met. He'd never felt the need to try to impress her, to try to pretend he was something other than exactly who he was. She listened when he talked. She cared about what he said. And she laughed. Ginny had a wonderful laugh, a beautiful smile, and over the years she'd been generous in sharing both of those things.

He couldn't have said exactly when he'd come to feel these things for her, only that it seemed he'd battled against his feelings forever. He'd certainly never thought he'd be here, putting her baby girl to bed, while fighting the memory of Ginny, her skin still flushed from her bath, her scent so sweet, yet so incredibly seductive.

Marc's hand made one more slow circle on Hannah's back. Looking down, he saw that the baby had rolled over onto her stomach and tucked her knees up under her.

He brushed the back of his two fingers against her cheek, then against her hair. "Oh, Hannah. What am I going to do with you? What am I going to do with your mama?"

If he was smart, he'd stay away. But he had the job to think about, and he was torn. He didn't want to hurt Ginny or Hannah by taking on this task. Of course, they might well end up being hurt if he didn't do this. Because even if he chose not to investigate, someone else would be assigned—someone who might not take the care that he would.

"Marc?" Ginny called softly to him from downstairs. "Everything all right? Is Hannah asleep?"

"I'll be right down," he said.

The aroma of Mexican food hit him about halfway down the stairs. He heard a dinging sound that he assumed was from the microwave, then entered the kitchen to see her setting the table for two.

Ginny's back was to him, and he could see the flowery cotton material of her nightgown hanging beneath the bottom of her robe and skimming the floor as she moved. He tried very hard to keep his thoughts on food and not the woman beneath the clothing.

"She didn't give you any trouble?" Ginny asked.

He had to clear his throat before replying. "No."

"You handled her like a pro."

What could he say? He was enchanted with Hannah Reed, and it hadn't taken that much to entertain her. "She's a beauty. And a charmer. Joe would have been so proud, and so..."

Ginny went still for a moment, then took a long, shaky breath.

Marc swore softly. "I'm sorry. I shouldn't have said that."

"No." Ginny shook her head, her back still turned to him. "It's okay. Joe would have been very proud of her."

"I'm sorry I brought it up."

Ginny's head fell forward. Her hands brushed against her face. Marc stood frozen in his spot. He saw her shoulders shaking, thought he might hear the faint sound of her crying in the otherwise silent kitchen.

As much as he feared touching her, he couldn't hold himself back. He made the five steps across the kitchen to where she stood, then put his hands on her upper arms, supporting her, trying to show her that she wasn't alone.

"I miss him, too. Every day." He was right behind her, her neck no more than two inches from his nose. He smelled something old-fashioned and sweet—like flowers in the springtime. Ginny nodded her head at his words and the delicate curls that had escaped from the knot on her head brushed against his cheek. He could just imagine putting his mouth against the spot where her hair ended and her beautiful soft skin began.

His body threatened to betray him then, and he stepped back, just in time. Ginny whirled around, her body brushing his as she did. Then she settled back against the cabinets, about as far away from him as she could get. He noticed that her breathing was just as agitated as his, saw the pulse point pounding in her throat before he closed his eyes and looked away.

She had to feel the tension in the room as clearly as he did. This unspoken thing between them had come alarmingly close to being dragged out into the open, and he didn't think either of them was ready for that.

"I'm sorry," Ginny said, watching him closely now. "I didn't mean to turn all weepy on you."

"It's all right."

She shrugged, then continued. "Every time I think I'm done crying, I prove myself wrong."

"It hasn't been that long, Ginny. No one's trying to rush you through your grief, are they?"

"No. I just get impatient with myself at times."

"Why don't you give yourself a break?"

"I will. At least I'll try. It was just seeing you with Hannah like that. It made me think about how much she's missing right now. How much Joe's missing. They say a woman's touch, her voice, the things she has to give a child, are so different from the things a man has to give. Hannah's going to miss out on all those things. She's never going to have a father."

"She won't have Joe," he corrected, much as he hated the idea that came to him. "That doesn't mean she won't ever have a father."

Ginny shook her head and sighed. "We were together for so long. Ten years ... I can't imagine marrying someone else."

"Give it time," he said, knowing he'd go out of his mind thinking of her with yet another man. "You don't have to make everything right with her world today—or tomorrow."

"I know. I guess I just forget that sometimes. I want her to have ... everything. Absolutely everything."

Marc knew Ginny too well, knew exactly where this was coming from. "Especially the things you never had?"

"Yes."

"Then that's what you'll give her, Ginny. You'll give her the best of everything." He saw so clearly now what he couldn't believe he hadn't seen before. Ginny had longed for her father when she was growing up. And now he knew how much it would mean to her for Hannah to have a father who would be with her every day. The memory of a man long dead would not be enough.

She put her hand against his upper arm, lightly and briefly. The touch was searing. "Thank you. I hope you're right."

"In this, I am." He waited, hating the fact that she would find a father for Hannah someday.

What in the world was he going to do then?

"Marc?" she asked.

He turned back to her, the awkwardness of that near caress slowly fading, the moment lost. He worked hard at clearing his throat. "So...something smells good."

They sat and ate, talking like old times, forgetting the strain of the previous moments. Ginny was clearly tired, but she swore she enjoyed having a grown-up to talk to at the end of the day.

Their meal finished, Marc thought he might get away, bloodied but unbowed. Then Ginny turned all serious on him again as he started to make his way to the back door. She stopped him by stepping into his path.

"You said you would help me, if you could."

"Yes."

Clearly uncomfortable, she leaned against the wall and sighed. "There are some things I need to know—about Joe."

Marc went still, watched her and waited. Ginny crossed her arms, looked at the floor, then the ceiling, then the wall. Anywhere except at Marc.

"Ginny? What is it?"

Still avoiding his eyes, she said, "Joe's mother won't talk about it at all. His father isn't much better. Even his uncles, the cousins, no one will tell me. And I have to know.''

''Know what?''

''Why did he die? What was he doing there that day? How did he get dragged into that mess?''

''Ginny...I...'' What could he say? He wanted to know the same things.

''Please,'' she said. ''Just hear me out. I still wonder about so many things. Was it just an accident? Just some strange, cruel twist of fate? Did he simply step onto that street at exactly the wrong time? Is that *really* all it was?''

Marc didn't say anything at first. He couldn't. He'd never imagined she'd ask him about any of this, and he realized now that he had no idea what the Reeds might have told her, or even what they really knew.

''You were his partner,'' she said when he didn't reply. ''You were there.''

''No. I wasn't.'' He closed his eyes, feeling again the helplessness, the rage.

''When you came to the house that day, you had blood on your shirt—Joe's blood.''

''Yes, but I got to the scene after he'd already been shot. I didn't see anything actually happen.''

''Oh.'' The sound was not much more than a soft rush of air from her lungs. She sank back against the wall and looked away again.

''Ginny, I don't know if this is a good idea.''

''Don't treat me like a child, Marc. I'm the same age as you.''

''I know.''

''And don't tell me you don't want to upset me. I lost my husband. Of course it's upsetting to me. But I need to know what happened. Why was he there, Marc?''

''I don't know.''

"You both were on duty."

"And I should have been there," he said quietly, bitterly, his words underscored by the rage that still hit him full-force at times. He swore and turned away.

"I didn't mean it that way," she insisted. "I wasn't blaming you."

"Well, maybe I blame myself." He felt defeated and utterly useless. Joe was gone. And he was still here, in Joe's house... wanting Joe's wife.

"Are you trying to tell me that this was somehow your fault?" Ginny asked. "Because I don't believe that, not for a minute."

Marc shook his head. This was his problem, not Ginny's. She was searching for a whole other set of answers. "I'm sorry," he said. "I shouldn't take this out on you."

"He wouldn't blame you."

"I know. But if I had been the one who died," he said bitterly, "and Joe hadn't been there, he would have blamed himself. You know that as well as I."

"So there's more than enough guilt to go around in this room," Ginny said.

"You, too?" At her tearful nod, he asked, "Why? What did any of this have to do with you?"

She put out her hand and he caught it, held it and waited. He could feel her trembling. He longed to take her into his arms, but he didn't dare.

"I can't go into that part of it. Not tonight, okay?"

He nodded.

"Will you still help me?"

"If I can."

"Tell me what you know."

Marc took a minute to collect his thoughts. He relived this almost daily and had to work to recite the facts calmly, without the pain that constantly plagued him.

"We were out half the night before on a homicide, and we got started a little late that morning. I was at the station house and Joe was out taking care of some sort of errand when the call came in about the shooting at the apartment." Marc shrugged helplessly. He was *assuming* Joe had been in the car and simply heard the radio call, but that bothered him. Everything about that day, everything he didn't know bothered him. "I'm sorry, Ginny."

"So, he just answered a call?"

"It looks that way."

"But you're not sure?"

"I don't think there's any way to be sure." He didn't like withholding the truth from her this way. But in the strictest sense of the word, this was the truth—he simply didn't know.

"Someday, Hannah's going to want to know what happened to her father. What am I going to tell her?"

Marc was silent.

"I think...something was going on...before he died."

Marc swore and looked away. Ginny was watching him much too closely for his own comfort.

"You saw it, too," she insisted.

"I don't know. I don't know what I saw." God help him, he didn't.

"He was different, Marc. Something happened, and he had changed. Something was bothering him, and he wouldn't talk to me about it. He didn't talk to you, either?"

Marc did not want to be having this conversation with Ginny Reed, even though the boys at headquarters would be thrilled that she'd chosen to confide in him. She was handing him the opportunity to do the job he'd been given to do and hadn't wanted. The irony amazed him.

"You said you'd help me," Ginny reminded him. "You could find out the truth. You were his partner and his friend."

"Ginny, you need to think about this. Think very carefully about what you're asking me."

"I have thought about it, and I'm sure. I have to know," she assured him. "Will you do this, Marc? For me?"

He closed his eyes. Ginny, Marc, the department—they all wanted the same answers, yet Marc was loath to uncover the truth for them. Still, it seemed the decision had been made.

No one could do this job better than he. No one else had his connections to Joe and to Joe's family. The Reeds would open up to him, as they would never open up to an outsider.

Only he could find the truth. He just prayed that the truth would not bring Ginny any more pain than she'd already been forced to endure.

Chapter 4

After saying a quick goodbye to Ginny, Marc drove to a coffee shop five blocks from her house and called O'Connor. The internal affairs officer agreed to meet with him that night.

While Marc waited, he thought about all he knew regarding the case.

Six days before Joe Reed had been shot and killed, a woman named Renata Leone had been murdered. Her throat had been slit, and her body left in an alley, where the authorities didn't discover it for several days. The man who had killed her, William Welsh Morris, had been her lover. He had also been a cop, a dirty one.

Holed up inside that apartment building the day Joe was killed had been the dead woman's eight-year-old son, Rico. The boy had come upon Morris not long after his mother was murdered. Rico had been hiding, in fear for his life, and the people helping to hide him had been in touch with the FBI. Some agents had been at the apartment that morning to take custody of the boy, but before they could do that, disaster had struck. Someone had tipped off Morris, and Morris had been waiting in the street, no doubt in hopes of silencing the boy, just as he'd silenced the mother.

The woman's son had escaped unharmed that day. But there had been a shoot-out between the FBI, Morris, and a policeman who apparently responded to the reports of shots being fired. Joe Reed had been that policeman, and he had died that day.

Had Joe known what was going down ahead of time? Had he knowingly put himself into the middle of that situation? And, if so, why?

Internal affairs had become suddenly interested now in investigating Joe. But the investigation couldn't have come at a worse time. Chicago was about to try police officer William Welsh Morris for the murder of another policeman. Suddenly all the hostility of cops faced with the gathering of evidence against one of their own had surfaced again. Joe Reed's death would be investigated within that climate of anger, fear and hatred. It was a dangerous combination. Still, for Marc, there was no backing out.

"I'll do it," he told O'Connor as the man took a seat beside him in a booth in back of the nearly deserted restaurant.

"Good." O'Connor hid his surprise well.

Marc knew Ginny wouldn't understand if she found out what he was doing. But this wasn't about the two of them. Marc was doing this for Ginny and for Joe, for Hannah and the entire family.

Because he was a fair-minded man, he asked himself if he was also doing it for himself. Partly because he wanted answers himself, but also because this would give him a reason to see Ginny. He was honest enough with himself to admit that he very much wanted to see Ginny, even though he knew seeing her often would only make things more difficult.

Still, Marc was determined. He was going to do whatever it took to prove Joe's innocence.

And if his work proved Joe's guilt? Marc was a cop; cops were taught to consider all the possibilities. He had to consider that one.

If he was the man who proved Joe guilty, Ginny would hate him. The whole family would hate him.

He would take that risk. He was betting on Joe's innocence.

"So, what do you want me to do?" he asked O'Connor. "And what do you people have on Joe Reed?"

"I want you to do what any good friend of the family would do. I want you to hang close, keep your ears open, ask questions when you can without arousing suspicion."

Marc's stomach clenched into a tight knot. Put that way, it sounded so unfeeling. He was anything but unfeeling here. Still, he managed to nod in agreement.

"I know this isn't going to be easy on you," the man said. "But you and Ginny are the same age. You grew up together, and I need someone she knows and trusts, someone who can get close to her without anyone becoming suspicious."

Marc laughed, injecting absolutely no humor into the sound.

"But it has to be done," O'Connor went on. "And remember, this investigation goes on with or without you. If you refuse to be a part of it, we'll find someone else. And we don't know if that person will be nearly as interested in proving Joey innocent."

"Believe me, I've thought of that."

"And I don't think I have to tell you that you can't let anyone in the family know what we're doing. You do that, and everything closes down to us. We won't get any information out of them quietly. And if we have to go public with this, Joey will be convicted based on the questions and the allegations alone. Once the media gets through with him, it won't matter whether he was guilty or not. And the family will never forgive either one of us for that."

Marc nodded. He understood all the complications very well.

"One more thing—let's be clear on this. I'm not asking you to prove to me that Joe Reed was innocent. I want the truth. I have to know that you're after the truth, as well. I'll want your word on that," O'Connor said solemnly.

"And you've got it."

"I'm not scared of the truth," O'Connor continued. "I just happen to believe that the truth is going to set Joey free."

Marc thought about the changes he'd seen in his partner toward the end. Joe had grown a strange detachment that he wore like a shield. One of the times he broke through the barrier, Joe had been temperamental, even downright rude. He'd gone on a lot of unexplained errands alone on police time, and he wouldn't give Marc the first clue as to where he was going or why it was so important to him.

Joe should have been with Marc that final morning, not off on another of his unexplained errands, not in the middle of a shoot-out in broad daylight.

So Marc couldn't say he had no fear of the truth in this case. But he definitely wanted to find out what the truth was.

"I won't lie to you," he promised O'Connor. "And I won't cover up anything, either."

"Son, I know you won't. Otherwise I never would have chosen you for this job."

"Now," Marc said, "my turn. What do your people have on Joe Reed?"

"Just enough to want to ask some questions."

"You're going to have to do better than that, O'Connor. It's about the trial, isn't it?" Marc could only speculate on that.

A year had passed and still the case hadn't come to trial, although that wasn't such a surprise given the volume of cases before the courts. Marc knew the prosecutor had decided to try Morris first for Joe's murder, rather than the murder of Renata Leone. Given the fact that the chief prosecution witness against Morris was a nine-year-old boy and that little evidence had ever been found in the Renata Leone case, Marc could understand that. He also understood the politics of the situation. Morris had killed a cop, and the public, as well as the police department, wanted to see someone pay for that.

This problem might be nothing more than a prosecutor being overly cautious going into a high-profile murder trial. And it might be something else entirely.

O'Connor hedged and admitted nothing.

Marc was getting madder every minute, just thinking about it. "That man who shot Joe, Morris, is pure scum, and he's coming to trial. He'd say anything to get off."

"I know."

"He won't walk on this. We've got the weapon that fired the bullet that killed Joe. We've got the killer's fingerprints on the weapon. We've got federal agents as witnesses who put Morris on the scene, firing a weapon. He can't get off with that kind of evidence against him.''

"No," O'Connor said, "but it would be to his advantage to throw as much confusion and speculation into this trial as he can.''

"With what?''

"Joe's gun, for one.''

"He got off a shot.'' Marc knew that already. "How's that going to help Morris?''

"It singed an FBI agent's right ear and landed in the wall of an apartment building behind the agent. We dug that bullet out of the wall. Ballistics is positive it came from Joe's gun.''

"It doesn't mean anything," Marc argued. "You couldn't tell the good guys from the bad out there that day.''

"It may not mean anything, but it could be made to imply a whole hell of a lot in court.''

Marc couldn't believe that. At least he didn't want to believe that. "We're talking about the word of a cop standing accused of slitting a woman's throat and fatally shooting another cop. A jury has to understand that he'll say anything.''

"Which makes him very dangerous.''

"Still, it's sheer desperation talking," Marc said.

"But that doesn't mean we can discount the potential impact of what he says. He gets up in court and says something to the effect that Joey was dirty, that he was there helping Morris go after the boy, not because of any radio call about shots being fired, and this whole thing is over. It's blown up in our faces. Joey isn't a fallen hero anymore—he's just a dirty cop who got shot while trying to kill a little boy to keep the kid from talking.

"And then the whole complexion of Morris's trial changes," O'Connor continued. "Juries hate cop-killers, but they're not so offended by a crook getting blown away in the middle of a shoot-out with the FBI and the police. Morris just bought himself life in prison rather than a death sentence. Hell, the guy could be out on parole in twenty years. And all he had to do was make up a few stories about Joey. It's a piece of cake."

Marc swore. O'Connor was right. It would be just that easy, and Morris was just that desperate.

"How long do we have before the trial starts?"

"Our best guess . . . maybe four weeks, if we're lucky. Depends on when it comes up on the court docket and whether the prosecutor's office can stall any more than it already has."

Four weeks? Marc swore again. It just kept getting worse and worse. And Ginny Reed was going to get caught up in the middle of this mess in one short month.

Not if I have anything to say about it, Marc promised himself.

He thought about Hannah—sweet, innocent little Hannah. Ginny was right. She'd want to know everything she could about her father someday. Marc wanted to find the answers for her. He wanted to be sure the picture she had in her mind was that of a man she could be proud of, that of a hero felled in the line of duty.

He would do anything to give those things to Hannah, just as he'd do anything to give them to Ginny.

Anything except lie.

And he had to remember, in taking on this job and knowing he'd never lie about anything he discovered, he just might be the man who proved to the entire city that Joe Reed was not a fallen hero, that he was in truth nothing more than a dirty cop.

Marc wasn't sure how he would live with himself then.

* * *

He called Ginny later that night, before he had a chance to reconsider. She answered on the third ring, her voice soft and smooth and sexy in a way that had the muscles in his stomach tightening and his heart skipping a beat or two.

"I woke you? I can call back," he said, unable to see anything in his mind except her in bed in whatever she'd been wearing under that robe tonight. The swiftness and the clarity of that image had every nerve in his body standing on end.

Before Hannah's baptism, he hadn't seen Ginny in months. And then a few hours spent in her company had brought him to this.

"It's all right," Ginny murmured sleepily, "Hannah's probably going to wake me soon, anyway. She's like a tanker truck, and I just can't keep her filled up."

"I've been thinking about what you asked me to do," he said softly. "Ginny...what if these things I find out...what if they're bad?"

"I'm prepared to take that chance," she said. "I didn't ask on a whim. I've been thinking about this for a long time. I just wasn't sure who I could ask to help me."

He understood that she wouldn't want to ask anyone in the family, and that she needed someone in the department. There weren't a lot of people who fit the bill. Still, he was glad she'd asked him.

"I'll do whatever I can," he promised her.

"Thank you, Marc. It means a great deal to me."

He said nothing. He didn't want her thanks, just a little understanding when this was all over.

"You need to be clear on this," Ginny said. "I want the truth, even if it does hurt."

It was an eerie echo of O'Connor's words to him earlier that day. "All right," Marc promised her, as he'd promised the IAD detective.

"I trust you, Marc."

He flinched at her words. All this talk about trust and the truth hit too close to home tonight. He thought of telling her about his assignment, then reconsidered. Ginny might never need to know about the IAD investigation— never worry or be hurt by it. He could shield her from that. And maybe someday she would see it that way—that he'd protected her from some of the ugliness and the unfairness surrounding her husband's death, instead of withholding the truth from her.

"You didn't tell me a lot tonight," Marc forced himself to continue. "You didn't tell me exactly why you're worried. You're going to have to do that, Ginny. You'll have to tell me everything."

"I know. I will."

From the tone of her voice, he wondered what she could possibly know. But this wasn't something to get into right this minute. He would ask his questions face-to-face, as a policeman did, not over the phone, late at night, with visions of a Ginny in her bed filling his head and taking his mind off the job at hand.

"So," he said, "we can get started tomorrow? After dinner, maybe?"

"Come by when you finish work. Have dinner with Hannah and me."

Already he saw the complications, but he agreed, then had to fight to make himself say goodbye and hang up the phone.

Marc was late. He'd called, insisted that it was nothing, but saying he'd be tied up long enough that he'd miss dinner. Ginny, a cop's wife for too long, tried not to worry and to wonder about what was keeping him.

Instead, she stayed busy around the house. She ate—alone—then let the pot of stew cool so that she could put it in the refrigerator. She gave Hannah a bath, dressed her in her footie pajamas, fed her and put her to bed. Ginny straightened up the house, checking the clock every fifteen minutes or so and telling herself not to imagine things.

Still, however irrational it was, she thought Marc must be in trouble. She watched the street out front, because she would be scared to answer the doorbell if it rang. She remembered too well what it was like to go to the front door and find the worst of all possible news waiting there. She wanted to see Marc coming from the car, so that she wouldn't have to wonder if he was all right in that eternity of seconds it took her to reach the door after the bell rang.

She fought the urge to pull out the police scanner and turn it on, just to reassure herself that nothing unusual was happening tonight. Ginny had broken herself of that habit years ago. The police scanner was a cop's wife's worst enemy. Something was always going on in a city this size, and listening to the police radio made it all too easy to imagine a family member or a loved one in the midst of whatever problem had surfaced at the moment.

Ginny had stopped listening after the first four years of her marriage. She couldn't go back to listening now.

Still, she was worried. She'd forgotten this feeling of sitting in a darkened house, waiting and watching for a man to come in off the streets. When she wasn't worrying about the danger Marc faced every day, she thought maybe he simply didn't want to come here tonight. Maybe she'd made him uncomfortable last night. Standing there in the kitchen with him, she'd felt something, something traitorous and illogical, something that robbed her of her sleep and left her examining her own motives.

Marc was a friend. He was someone she could trust, someone who could keep a secret, and he was loyal to Joe yet wasn't a member of the family. When he walked into Hannah's bedroom the night of the baptism, Ginny had known she'd made the right choice.

There'd always been a special bond between the two of them, ever since they were teenagers, both lonely and longing for a family like the Reeds. But was that all it was? Two kids wanting the same thing? Two people on the edge of a family who wanted desperately to belong?

In the kitchen last night, for a moment, it had felt like something else entirely, something that seemed to have a power and an energy all its own. It had felt like some man-to-woman connection that, after all her years with Joe, she must have forgotten.

Ginny had been a little shocked by the feelings at first, and now she'd grown wary of them. Surely she'd simply made too much of nothing. After all, she'd been alone for a long time now. She hadn't been anywhere near a man— a man who wasn't part of the family—since Joe had been killed.

Marc was an attractive man. She was a lonely woman. So, there had been a little spark between them last night. Maybe that just meant the woman inside her hadn't disappeared forever beneath her widow's weeds.

Still, if Marc had noticed... If she'd made him feel uncomfortable... Even worse, if he felt sorry for her... How would she face him again? Ginny's cheeks flamed just at the thought.

Ginny went to the window, pulled back the old-fashioned lace curtains and studied the street, again finding it empty. She sighed and tried to put her mind on the problem at hand, then heard a car approaching and slowing.

She held her breath until the car door swung open and she saw Marc climb out and head for the house. Telling herself she was being ridiculous, she went to open the door before he rang the bell and woke Hannah.

Marc looked up, startled, as his hand was reaching for the bell, and then he stepped back.

"Hi." Ginny thought he looked tired and a little uneasy. She forced a smile across her lips, despite her worries.

"Sorry I'm late," he said, looking down at his watch. "I didn't even check to see how late it was. If you like, I can come back tomorrow instead."

"No, this is fine." She held open the door. "Come inside. Is everything all right?"

He stepped across the threshold. "We just . . . ran into a situation that took longer than I expected to clear up."

Ginny smiled at that. "Cop talk for 'Ask me no questions, I'll tell you no lies.'"

"What?" he said softly, all his attention on her now.

"I only meant that I should have known better than to ask what was going on. I know there are a lot of things involved with the job that a detective can't explain to anyone. I didn't mean to put you on the spot."

"Oh . . . sorry. It's been a long day."

"Did you stop to eat dinner?"

"I had a sandwich."

"When?"

"Around five."

"And now it's after nine. Come on into the kitchen. I'll put some of the stew in the microwave."

"You don't have to do that," he said, following her down the hallway and into the kitchen. "Especially since I stood you up."

"I know I don't have to, but I'm offering anyway. You're tired. You're hungry. And you just happen to be in my kitchen. I might as well feed you."

She busied herself with the stew, finding a microwavable dish, finding a spoon, searching for a cloth napkin.

Marc seemed a little on edge, and she was trying not to let that worry her. He'd worked late. He was probably just edgy about whatever case he was on.

He ate two bowls of stew while she sipped her tea and watched him. She'd promised to tell him everything, yet now that the time had come, she was finding it difficult.

Ginny told herself to snap out of it. Marc was one of Joe's closest friends, too. She'd have bet that if he didn't know what Joe had been up to, he at least had his suspicions. She would just have to be the one who brought this out into the open.

The time for protecting Ginny Reed, for keeping secrets from her and for deciding what was best for her, was over. Those decisions were hers now. Marc would have to understand that.

"Hey..." he said softly.

She turned, finding him standing beside her and not knowing how long he'd been standing there.

"Something's on your mind," he said.

"Joe."

Marc nodded. "I guess it's time to talk."

Ginny nodded. "Come into the living room. The sofa's much more comfortable than the kitchen chair. Would you like some coffee?"

He shook his head and followed her once again. Ginny took one end of the sofa. He took the other. She sat worrying with the fingers of her hand and trying to think of how to start.

"It's harder than I thought it would be," she admitted.

"Take your time."

She shrugged, knowing her time was up. "The Reeds...they've been treating me like spun glass since Joe's death. I swear, if they could have, they would have wrapped me in a cocoon the whole time I was pregnant with Hannah. Losing Joe like that, then finding out I was pregnant...after all the false hopes, all the trying."

Ginny stopped. She hated discussing her fertility problems, hated to put such a simple label on a mountain of heartache. So she didn't talk about them to anyone, not anymore. But she suspected Joe and the family did. "You knew what we went through trying to have a baby?"

"Yes."

Ginny closed her eyes and was grateful he didn't say anything else. "Anyway," she continued, "with my medical history, we weren't sure I could carry Hannah to term. Mama Reed and the doctor kept telling me I had to stay calm, for the baby's sake. So right from the start they closed in around me, not letting anyone get close to me. They unplugged the TV so I didn't hear the news. Unplugged the radios. Stopped the newspaper delivery without telling me, and I swear, I was in such a fog, four months passed before I even missed my morning paper.

"They hardly told me anything about what happened that day. And at first I didn't care. It didn't matter. Joe was gone. Nothing was going to bring him back. Knowing the answers wouldn't have helped.

"I tried to concentrate all my energies on my pregnancy, once I finally let myself believe that everything was going to work out and I was really going to have a baby.

And after she came, I was so exhausted and so busy, I hardly had time to do anything—even ask questions—until now."

Ginny paused, still amazed herself at how long this had gone on. "It's hard to believe a whole year has passed. But that's over. Now, I want to know. I have to."

"All right. I'll tell you what I can."

"And help me find the answers to the questions you can't answer yourself?"

"Yes," he said. "Ginny, is this about the trial?"

"Partly."

"You don't want to go sit there every day, Ginny. I know the prosecutors want you there, so the jury can see the grieving widow, but you don't want to put yourself through that every day."

"I'm going. I want to see that man. I want him to see me. I want him to know what he's done to me and to my child."

"Ginny—"

She held up her hand, as if that alone could distance her from the whole experience. "Regardless of whether or not I'm there, I'm going to hear about it. I don't want to find out my husband's secrets for the first time in front of the jury and the reporters, the Reeds, and whoever happens to be in the courtroom that day. Surely you can understand that?"

"I can."

"Okay." She took a deep breath to steady herself. She'd been dreading this moment. She hated feeling this awful sense of helplessness, this humiliation, over all these things she could not change. "Joe and I . . . we had our problems. I don't know how much he told you. . . ."

Marc shrugged and shook his head. "He told me about how hard you two were trying to have a family."

"That's all?"

"More or less. But what does this have to do with his death?"

"I'm getting to that part." But she couldn't resist asking, "What else did he tell you?"

"Ginny, what's the point?"

"I never got to talk to him at the end. I know how we left things as he walked out the door that morning, and then it was over. We never got to clear up anything between us, never resolved anything. If only I could have had five minutes with him. Just five minutes."

Marc's hand reached out across the cushions of the sofa and settled over hers. Ginny didn't cry, because if she started, she'd never be able to stop. "What did he tell you about me? And about our marriage?"

"Don't do this," Marc said.

"I can't ask him."

"He said more than anything else you wanted a baby, and he was afraid he'd never be able to give you one."

She turned sharply. "He said that?"

Marc didn't look at her. Instead, he stared straight ahead, at the opposite wall. Everything about the way he held himself told her he did not want to be having this conversation with her. But he was going to help. He'd made her a promise.

"It wasn't Joe's fault," she explained. "We had all the infertility tests. He was fine."

"He never said anything about that."

"But why would he blame himself?"

"It's a man thing, Ginny. You were his wife, you were unhappy, and he couldn't fix that."

"Really?"

"It's what a man does—he makes the woman he loves happy."

"I never thought of it that way. I just thought he didn't want to have a child as much as I did. He used to get so angry, just talking about it."

"That was his pride talking—the part of him that wasn't able to give you what you wanted."

"I'd like to believe that," Ginny said. With all her heart, she longed to believe it was as simple as that. "But the truth is, I think he was going to leave me."

"Oh, Ginny..." Marc slid across the sofa until he was right beside her. Then he turned her shoulders until she faced him. "Joe would never have left you."

Ginny looked at Marc's plain white dress shirt, at the plain white buttons, the texture of the light brown suit jacket, anywhere but at him. This was even harder than she'd expected.

"Joe was different the last few months before he died," Ginny told him. "You saw that yourself. At the end, he was tense, impatient, short-tempered. It was as if he were wrapped up in his own little world, and there was no room for me anymore. But I think... I think he made room for someone else."

"What?"

She flinched at the power behind that word. "I think there was another woman. And I think Joe was going to leave me for her."

"Ginny, that's crazy."

"He was always sneaking out of the house, staying out late, saying it was work when I always found out it wasn't. He ran all sorts of errands, made lots of phone calls he never explained. How do you account for that?"

"I can't, but I know that Joe Reed loved you. He had since he was a kid, and he never stopped."

Love?

She shook her head sadly. "Marc, sometimes love isn't nearly enough."

Chapter 5

Marc did not want to hear these kinds of things about Joe and Ginny's marriage. He realized his grip on her shoulders was so tight it was a miracle her bones hadn't snapped under the pressure. And he had to fight to make himself let go, because he needed some distance between the two of them before he hauled her into his arms.

It hurt so much to think of her suffering this way that, for a minute, he felt as if someone had split open his chest and laid his heart bare.

Sometimes love isn't nearly enough.

Well, surely he already knew that. Despite all he felt for Ginny, nothing had changed because of it. Unless he counted Joe's death as some sort of twisted answer to his prayers. Of course, God didn't answer prayers like that. And Marc had certainly never prayed for Joe's death. He'd simply felt much too much for Joe's wife.

The only thing Marc could say in his defense was that he'd never acted on those feelings, and he prayed that he'd never given Joe any reason to suspect what he felt. Joe had certainly never indicated in any way that he might know, except there at the very end, when he asked Marc to take care of Ginny.

Now that Marc thought about it, he'd never told Ginny that her husband's last words had been for her. He'd told the family simply that before he died Joe's last thoughts had been of Ginny.

Marc tried to remember exactly what he'd told the investigators later. Had he recalled Joe's actual words for them? Or had he simply said that Joe hadn't mentioned anything about who shot him and he'd been too shaken up to ask? Marc honestly couldn't remember. And he didn't like the idea of Joe's last words to him coming out for the first time in court.

So he would have to tell Ginny. Knowing now what she suspected about Joe, he could just imagine the kind of slant she would put on her husband's last words.

It wasn't true, Marc's gut instincts told him. Joe Reed hadn't been fooling around with anyone. And he would never have left Ginny—not voluntarily, anyway.

"Ginny," Marc got up and walked across the room, "he loved you. There is absolutely no doubt in my mind."

"He talked about leaving."

He whirled back to face her. "What?"

"The night before he died." She stopped to take a breath. "He said something about needing some space. Barbara was driving to Cincinnati for a cousin's wedding that weekend, and he kept saying how much Barbara and I enjoyed each other's company. He wanted me to go, but I didn't. I was too scared of what was happening between us to leave."

"You're making too much of that."

"No," she insisted. "When I wouldn't go, he said that maybe he'd go someplace for a couple of days, just to get his head on straight."

"It's not what you think." Marc was positive of that.

Ginny swallowed hard and nodded. "He was going to leave me."

"No. You've misread the whole thing."

"Marc, we hadn't been happy in years. Joe was right. I can see it now, so clearly. I was so consumed by the idea of having a baby that it blinded me to everything else. And the stress involved with infertility is enormous. The medical tests, the money, the heartbreak of the miscarriage—I didn't have anything left for Joe. And he would just shut down to the point where I couldn't tell how he felt. Or if he felt anything. And toward the end, the anger started. Maybe it was just frustration—I don't know. I couldn't tell, and he certainly wasn't volunteering any information."

"I still think you're wrong."

Marc watched as she shook her head and wrapped her arms around herself. Ginny looked so lonely and so brokenhearted, it made him ache inside and out.

Marc wanted to go to her now, to offer what little comfort he could. But he was afraid to touch her. He wasn't sure how he'd make himself let her go.

Worst of all, a part of him was wondering if she hadn't just handed him some sort of clue internal affairs might find interesting. Certain things motivated men into incredibly stupid actions. Greed. Jealousy. Anger. Fear. And sex. A lot of men did incredibly stupid things because of sex.

If Joe had another woman, that brought up a whole string of possibilities Marc had never considered.

Could Morris have found out about Joe's mistress and been blackmailing him in some way? Would Joe have gone so far as to help a dirty cop to keep Ginny from finding out about his mistress?

Not if he was planning to leave her, Marc argued with himself.

Still, there were possibilities. Could this mystery woman of Joe's somehow be tied to Morris's dirty dealings? So far, the only woman known to have been involved was Renata Leone, and she was dead. They had good information, from Renata's own son, that Morris had been Renata's boyfriend. And Morris had been charged with Renata's murder as well. Renata's son had said nothing about Joe Reed.

But that didn't mean there wasn't a second woman involved.

It was possible. Marc had been a cop long enough to know that almost anything was possible. But it certainly didn't seem probable, not to someone who had known Joe Reed and worked with him day in and day out for six years.

Still, his job was to do what internal affairs sent him here for, to find out information just like this—even if it did leave a sour taste in his mouth.

Marc made himself walk back to Ginny, who was sitting on the sofa. He saw the tears falling down her cheeks, watched as she hastily wiped them away, then turned her face toward the opposite wall.

"Are you sure you want to go through with this?" he said, half hoping she would say no.

Ginny nodded. "That was the hardest part, and it's done now."

"So you want me to go find out if your husband was involved with another woman?"

She shrugged indecisively. "I have this image in my mind of myself at the trial, hearing for the first time that he was on his way to see some other woman when he got shot. I don't want to come face-to-face with her in the courtroom and have her tell me my husband was in love with her and leaving me for her. And...well, I hate to even mention this, but...I've been hearing rumors."

Jeez, this just kept getting worse. "Rumors?" he said, his tone as even as he could make it.

"About Joe and the cops who were arrested. Don't pretend you haven't heard them, too."

"You stay in this business long enough, you hear every rumor in the world."

"But you've heard this one about Joe?"

As Marc saw it, there was no possibility of getting out of this. She'd heard the rumors. Still, maybe he could ease her mind a little. "Ginny, you know how paranoid people get when cops start getting arrested. And you know what the rumor mill at the station is like."

"You don't believe it, do you?"

"No."

"No doubts?"

Marc swore, then apologized for that. "He was different at the end, just as you said. And I don't know why. I don't believe it was another woman. I don't believe he was a dirty cop. I think there's another explanation for that. I think there's the truth, and that will explain everything."

"Find it for me? Find out the truth?"

"I will."

"Thank you. I can't tell you how much this means to me, how much it will mean to Hannah someday."

"I would do anything I could to help you. Anything at all. Remember that, okay?"

She nodded.

"So, how am I going to go about finding this nonexistent woman? Do you have any idea who she might be? A name, nickname, phone number? Anything?"

Ginny shook her head. "He talked to someone on the phone, and he wouldn't tell me who it was."

"Are you sure it was a woman?"

"No, but what else could it be? He kept saying it was a case, but you all weren't working on any big case that intently for weeks on end, were you?"

Marc took a minute to think about whether there was any case that Joe had taken a particular interest in around that time. "We had unsolved cases. Everyone does. But you're right. We didn't have anything big where something had shaken loose recently. At least nothing he told me about."

"And he would have told you. You were his partner."

"It seems he would have told me."

"So what else could it be?"

"I don't know. But I'm going to find out." And he would. One way or another.

"Even if you think I'd be better off not knowing?"

He glanced away, knowing there was no right answer to that one.

"I'm not a child."

"And Mama Reed hasn't quite figured that out?"

"Either that or she and a lot of other people seem to think widowhood is somehow linked to incompetence. It's like I'm the only woman in the world who was ever faced with raising a child alone." Ginny paused to reconsider. Lowering her voice, she said, "I'm not nearly as fragile as they seem to think I am."

"I know that."

"And I can handle the truth. Whatever it is."

The truth? Well, there was one truth he hadn't owned up to yet, and it was one that would never come easily to her. If he wanted to keep her trust, he had to tell her now, even though he could imagine what kind of slant Ginny would put on this.

"Look," he said, "there's something else I have to tell you, about the day Joe was shot. When I said I got there too late, I meant I was too late to cover his back, maybe to prevent him from getting shot. But I made it to the scene before he died."

"You did?" She was wary now.

"He was still conscious when I got there."

Marc saw the tightening of her jaw, the harsh sound of her breathing, which she was struggling to control. And her back went ramrod-straight.

"You talked to him?" she asked.

"Yes."

"What... what did he say?"

"He was thinking about you."

"And?"

"He asked me to promise to take care of you, and I told him I would."

"That's it?"

Marc shook his head. "It's not what you think, okay?"

"What I'm thinking right now is scaring me. What did he say?"

"I think he knew that he was dying, that he was leaving you all alone, and he deeply regretted that."

Ginny shook her head back and forth. "His exact words—what were they?"

And then Marc couldn't hold the words back any longer. "He said, 'Tell Ginny, I'm sorry.'"

Ginny flinched as if she'd been struck. She clamped her hand over her mouth and managed not to make a sound. But the look on her face said it all.

"Dammit, Ginny. He wasn't apologizing because there was some other woman."

"You don't know that," she said.

"He could have meant a thousand different things. You said the two of you had problems toward the end. You said he talked about needing some space and wanting to move out for a while. He could have meant he was sorry about that."

"Maybe."

"Ginny, if you were the one who was dying that day, and if you had a few seconds and enough strength to speak just a few words to him, what would they have been?"

"That I loved him. And that..."

"Maybe that you were sorry? About all the tension between the two of you? Sorry about what not having a child did to your marriage? Sorry that you wouldn't have one more day together, one more hour, one more minute?"

Marc saw the first tears spill over the rim of her eyelids and fall down her cheeks. He saw her, so uncertain, so utterly alone, hurting so much. And he fought with everything he had to control his feelings for her, but the thing that drew him to her was stronger than either of them.

"Aw, Ginny," he said. And then he took her into his arms and just held on to her.

Here in Joe's house, talking about Joe's death and Joe's marriage, he felt like such a traitor. This wasn't what Joe had meant when he asked Marc to take care of his wife.

Traitor. The word rattled around inside his head, even as his mind registered the feel of Ginny in his arms, the trembling of her body, the smell of her hair, the hands that clung to him as he clung to her.

Traitor.

Both to her and to Joe.

He didn't know what was right. What was honorable. What should be done because it needed to be done and because he was the one who could best get the job done.

So what did he know? That he didn't want to let go of the woman in his arms. That he didn't want to tarnish her memories of her husband, and that he was afraid.

More than anything, he was afraid.

He'd rather face down a scared, unpredictable teenage gang member with a loaded machine gun than be the one to prove to Ginny Reed that her husband had been a crooked cop.

And then, there were his baser desires, as well. He'd thought he would be able to control his body's reaction to her, but he was failing miserably at that. She was like silk in his arms, soft, smooth and sensuous. At some point, her face had found its way to the hollow between his jaw and his shoulder. Her tears fell onto the side of his neck, and her breath skimmed across his skin, setting off little bursts of desire as it went.

"Ginny," he said, too sternly, almost jumping away from her, startling her and leaving him swearing and fighting for an ounce of control.

She stared at him as if she were trying to look right through his skin and into his heart and mind.

"I'm sorry," he said, because there wasn't anything else to say. And then he just turned away.

Hannah had impeccable timing for once. She started howling.

Ginny had never been so grateful to flee her own living room.

She thought of every depressing and upsetting thing she'd learned tonight. Joe had been doing something wrong before he died, and he'd used his dying breath to tell her he was sorry.

And something was happening between her and Marc. She couldn't be mistaken about that any longer.

When he held her in his arms...

"Oh, no..." Ginny told herself. She wasn't going to think about that right now, either. She couldn't. Maybe later, when Marc was gone, Hannah was asleep again and she could be alone.

Ginny made it to the door of Hannah's room. A quick glance at the clock showed that it was 10:45. Hannah was lying on her side, kicking her feet and waving her fists. The howling hadn't diminished one bit at the sound of her mother's voice.

"What is it, Hannah, my girl?"

Ginny lifted her from the crib and brought the baby to her chest. Hannah snuggled in and smacked her lips against her fist, but that didn't seem to soothe her. Ginny put her hands on Hannah's cheeks and saw the flush there. Her hand registered the heat coming off the baby, and the cold, clammy feel of her skin. Hannah's hair was damp with sweat, as was the back of her sleeper.

Her baby was burning up with fever.

Two hours later, after Ginny had woken Hannah's pediatrician, after she'd bathed the baby to bring down the temperature and after Marc had made a run to the supermarket for some over-the-counter medication, Hannah's fever was down. The only problem was, the baby was wide awake. It was nearly one o'clock in the morning. But Marc was still there, thank goodness.

Ginny was exhausted, and she could not stop shaking. Hannah had never been sick before. The doctor thought it was probably just an ear infection, but wanted Ginny to bring the baby to his office in the morning so that they would know for sure.

One little ear infection, and Ginny had been reduced to this—a mother practically paralyzed with fear. She had no idea what she would have done if Marc hadn't been here. Probably she would have made a near-hysterical phone call to Joe's mother. Then she would have heard again that she had no business living in this house alone and raising her daughter by herself when Joe had so many relatives in town who would be more than happy to take them in.

Well, Ginny didn't want to be taken in. She didn't want to live anywhere but here, in her own house, with Hannah.

But tonight, with nothing but a minor medical problem, she'd fallen apart. Marc had been the calm one.

Just having someone else in the house helped tremendously, but Ginny suspected that the fact that it was Marc mattered even more. He had Hannah in his arms right now, probably because he knew Ginny was still shaking too hard to hold her.

"Go to bed," Marc urged. "I'll sit with her until she goes to sleep."

"But you're on duty in the morning."

"And you have to take care of this little girl tomorrow. That certainly qualifies as work."

"I know, but I can't ask you to do that."

"Ginny, you didn't ask. I volunteered. Besides, Hannah likes me." He turned to the baby. "Don't you, sweet thing?"

Hannah grabbed his hair and pulled, then roared like an angry lioness with a thorn in her paw.

Marc winked at her and settled the two of them in the recliner. He leaned back in the chair and laid Hannah across his chest. "See? She does like me."

Ginny watched her daughter squirm for a minute, then burrow into the hollow between Marc's right arm and his side. Hannah tucked her head under Marc's chin, and one of her fists curled around the collar of his shirt. And then she started to make that cat sound, a little hum like a tiny motor running, a sound Ginny always associated with contentment.

"I think that settles that," Marc said. "Go on upstairs."

"You're sure you don't mind staying?"

"Ginny, go to bed."

And she went, falling into an exhausted sleep the instant her head hit the pillow.

Ginny woke disoriented and groggy. It took her a minute to remember what had happened the night before. Quickly she climbed out of bed and headed downstairs in search of Hannah.

She found her girl asleep with Marc in the recliner. With a heavy heart, Ginny watched the two of them for a minute and imagined another man's face relaxed in sleep, another man's arms wrapped protectively around the baby.

She was imagining another life, the one she and Hannah had been denied.

Her grief for Joe, at first overwhelming and all-consuming, had given way to more of a longing. She missed him. She yearned for him, for the early days when they had been so happy and for the future with Hannah that they would never share. She wanted the three of them to finally be a family, the kind she'd dreamed of having when she was a girl.

But watching Hannah now, Ginny had traitorous thoughts running through her head. Ginny wanted to give Hannah everything in the world she needed. And what was the most basic of things any child needed? Two parents. A father, as well as a mother.

Marrying again had seemed to be something so far out of the realm of possibility that Ginny dismissed it almost immediately. People had brought up the subject with Ginny as early as Joe's funeral. She was young, they'd say. She didn't want to be alone forever. She would find someone. She would fall in love again, or at least marry for companionship and to give Hannah a father.

It had made Ginny angry at first. And then she'd come to believe her stock answer—that she'd been married to Joe for so long she couldn't imagine being married to anyone else.

What had Marc said? That she would give Hannah everything, especially the thing she had most longed for and been denied?

Oh, Lord, Ginny thought. He was right. Raised by her maiden aunt after her parents' death, Ginny had longed for her mother, for a brother or a sister—and for a father. While she couldn't bring Joe back for Hannah, it was within her power to give Hannah a family of her own.

Ginny looked again at her daughter, curled up asleep against this kind, generous, loving man. For just a minute, she imagined that there was nothing at all unusual about finding him dozing in the recliner with her daughter.

She imagined another pregnancy, one she wouldn't endure alone, another birth, a myriad of rituals and firsts, like a baby's baptism, a first Christmas, a first tooth, first steps, first words.

She saw Hannah, her hair long now and flying behind her as she ran, saw another child, a boy, go careering after her on legs that weren't nearly as steady.

The joy within the dream image was so strong it was almost a painful thing, and it didn't seem as distant or as impossible as it once had.

Soon, the dream took on a vibrancy, a color and a texture all its own, to the point where it seemed real to her. And in the midst of this daydream, the man had a face and a name.

Marc.

Chapter 6

When Marc opened his eyes, he was alone in the recliner. His neck hurt, his head ached, and his arms were empty. From the smell that hit him the instant he opened his eyes, he knew someone was cooking. He sniffed again—bacon.

Groggily he checked his watch, saw that it was morning, but just barely.

The last thing he remembered was convincing Ginny to go to bed, then settling himself in the chair in the corner. Hannah had been cuddled up against him, squirming at times, whimpering, pouting, jibber-jabbering and tugging on her poor little ears.

He wondered how long he'd slept and how long Hannah had slept. Shoeless, tieless, his shirtsleeves rolled up, his hair shoved back with an impatient hand, he followed the smell of the bacon into the kitchen.

Standing over the stove was Ginny, wearing that soft pink terry-cloth robe—a garment that was starting to give him fits. There was nothing at all revealing about it. Yet he always felt as if he'd been caught staring at something he had no right to see.

"Morning."

She turned and gave him a smile, broken up a second later with a big yawn.

"I'm assuming you found your daughter, because I seem to have misplaced her."

"She woke up about forty-five minutes ago to eat, then went right back to sleep."

"So you're running on, what—about four hours' sleep?"

"I count myself lucky to have gotten that much. If you hadn't been here, I wouldn't have. I appreciate you staying."

He shrugged, as nonchalantly as he could. "It was the least I could do."

"It was more than that. Hannah's never been sick before, and I'm sure if I'd been alone when I took her temperature, I would have panicked and hauled her off to the emergency room. Then I would have been lucky to have gotten two hours' sleep. And there's no telling how much that trip to the hospital would have cost me."

"Ginny, money isn't a problem, is it?" He hadn't even considered that.

"We're fine," she said.

"You're sure?" She'd answered him so quickly and so vehemently that he doubted her all the more. He made a mental note to have a talk with one of the Reeds about the kind of financial situation Joe had left her in.

Ginny nodded. "I'm sure. I just would have hated to pay a couple hundred dollars for someone to tell me my daughter has an ear infection."

Which seemed perfectly reasonable to him. Still, he'd check. Because he didn't think he would get any more out of her about this particular subject, he dropped it, then asked, "Are you going to be all right here today? You've got to be exhausted."

"I'll nap this afternoon, when Hannah does."

"You mean *if* Hannah does."

"Oh, she will. Hannah likes her sleep. Maybe not in an eight-hour stretch during the night, like normal people, but she makes up for it during the day. We sleep away a lot of afternoons together."

She said it with a smile, but Marc still didn't like the reality of Ginny left here to raise this child alone. It made him feel guilty for having stayed away so long. "I think she's starting to grow on me. If you ever need help with her—and I don't care what time of the day or night—you call me, okay?"

Ginny nodded again.

"Remember, I'm living on Monroe now. I'm only about four blocks from here."

"I remember." She turned back to the stove. "I hope you still like bacon and scrambled eggs. I thought the least I could do was feed you before your shift starts."

"That's fine. It smells great."

"Ready for coffee?"

"Definitely." Marc sat down at the table while she poured him a cup. "How was Hannah when she woke up?"

"Fussy, but her fever was gone. The doctor said he'd work us in this morning at his office when we got there, so we don't have to rush. I'll let her sleep as long as she wants."

Marc had an urge to touch Ginny, one he didn't fight this morning. He turned and took her hand in his, then looked down at it, seeing the impression in her slightly tanned hand of a white band of skin that had once been covered by a plain gold wedding band. "I hate that you have to go through this alone. It makes me so damned mad."

Ginny stiffened. He felt the slightest bit of resistance as she tried to pull her hand away, and then she stopped fighting him. He had to stop touching her this way.

But it was too easy to reach for her, too tempting, too...impossible. This was impossible. If he was going to manage this job he'd been given, he had to learn to control his feelings for Ginny.

Still, seeing her last night, afraid, uncertain, all alone...it had nearly been his undoing. He'd done his best to help, without stretching the limits of friendship. But he wasn't sure how long he could make that work.

"I'm sorry," he said, but he didn't drop her hand. "I shouldn't have brought it up."

"No, it's okay. Sometimes I think I'm the only one who's angry because Joe's gone."

"It's just so unfair." Marc squeezed her hand gently, then told himself to let her go.

Just then, a knock sounded at the door. It opened before either of them had time to react.

"Ginny, how many times have I told you not to—" Jimmy Reed stopped in his tracks, his voice fading away in midsentence as he stared at them.

Marc dropped Ginny's hand and leaned back in the chair. Ginny had jumped about a mile when the door opened.

Jimmy recovered first. He advanced another step, toward Marc. "What the hell is going on here?"

"Don't jump to conclusions," Marc said. "Hannah got sick last night while I was here, and Ginny needed some help."

"If Ginny needs help, all she has to do is call her family and somebody will come running."

"Well, there was no need for that," Marc said. "I was already here, and happy to help out."

Jimmy obviously had other ideas about what had transpired. "It's six-thirty in the morning," he announced. "My baby brother's wife is in her bathrobe, and you—"

"Look like I've slept in my clothes, which I did. Don't be an ass, Jimmy."

"Now wait a minute."

"No, you wait a minute. Ginny's had about four hours' sleep. I think I've had less than that, because Hannah fussed all night, and neither one of us is in the mood for this today. I have to get to work, and Hannah has to go to the doctor. If you want to argue about this some more, you'll have to check with me later, okay?"

Jimmy said nothing.

"And don't go giving Ginny a hard time about this. Nothing happened."

"I still don't like this."

"And I don't like your implications."

Ginny jumped in. "Come on, Jimmy. You know Marc. He's like family."

Still Jimmy glared at the two of them. Marc felt even guiltier than before about every bit of attraction he'd ever felt for Ginny, and hoped the guilt didn't show in his face. Ginny stood by the stove and looked guilty enough for the two of them.

Finally Jimmy backed off. He said to Ginny, "Barbara wanted me to tell you that she can't make it over today, but that she'll call you later." And then, to Marc, he asked, "You're on duty this morning?"

"Yes."

Jimmy nodded. "We'll talk later."

Marc held his tongue. This wasn't the time or the place to have it out with Jimmy Reed. Ginny was upset enough.

Jimmy let himself out with one last quip. "And lock the door behind me."

The door closed behind Jimmy. Ginny made no move to lock it. Marc got up and did that himself, then stood with his back to the door. "I hate to admit it, but he's right about that. Surely you don't make a habit of leaving the back door unlocked."

"I went to get the paper! And now they're going to make a federal case out of that. I'll have three phone calls by noon on the perils of neglecting to lock my door. And that doesn't even begin to cover the calls I'll get about having a man in the house overnight or getting caught cooking breakfast for him in my robe, which covers more of me than any dress I own."

"Ginny, we both know we haven't done anything wrong."

"It doesn't matter what we have or haven't done."

"It's the only thing that does matter." Even if he had thought of at least a dozen things he'd like to do with this woman—kissing her being at the top of the list at the moment—they hadn't done anything.

And would it necessarily be wrong if they did share a kiss?

Marc had nothing but his conscience as his guide. And his conscience said kissing Ginny Reed would definitely be a guilt-provoking move.

"I think you'd better go." She turned back to the stove so that she didn't have to face him. "I'll make some toast and put together a sandwich for you. And I'll talk to you later, okay?''

Frustrated, but not wanting to push it at the moment, Marc agreed. ''Call me and let me know what the doctor says about Hannah?''

''Sure.''

He left it at that, because he had a visit from Jimmy Reed to look forward to, most likely a visit from Ben and a phone call from Mama Reed. That was just the barebones list.

Any man who ever came calling on Ginny Reed would be scrutinized within an inch of his life. Still, Marc envied that man.

Envied? Hell, he wanted to *be* that man.

The doctor said Hannah had an ear infection, something he assured Ginny was not at all uncommon in a child her age. He prescribed an antibiotic and sent them home.

Hannah was a little fussy, but not nearly as miserable as she had been the night before. Ginny nursed her around one o'clock, then put her down for a nap.

Downstairs, she dutifully checked the doors, found them all locked, checked the answering machine, found the message light blinking. She could just imagine the little jewels awaiting her there.

Ginny turned down the ringer on the phone, and was headed upstairs to take a nap herself when the doorbell rang.

''Coming,'' she called, bracing herself, even as she reminded herself how lucky she was to have so many people looking after her welfare and Hannah's. After all, she knew what it was like to be alone in this world.

"Barbara," she said, relieved that it was her ever-reasonable sister-in-law at the door. "What took you so long?"

The woman, even shorter than Ginny, and a little rounder, with dark hair and kind eyes, laughed as she walked inside. "Hey, I had to fight to get this assignment. Mama Reed wanted to come herself. Antonio and Christopher were especially livid. And Jimmy may still come by on his way home from work tonight, so brace yourself."

"I will, believe me. Come and sit down. I'm about to fall over if I don't get off my feet."

"So Hannah really is sick?"

"Yes, she's sick. Do you want a note from her doctor to prove it?"

"No, but it might help you save face with Mama Reed."

"Oh, Barb." Ginny tried to make light of it, but she couldn't pull it off. "Keep them away from me, please. I'm too tired to handle them today, and I'd probably fly off the handle. There's no telling what I'd say."

"Look, I know nothing happened."

"Thank goodness someone does."

"And I know they're all being ridiculous."

"They are," Ginny said. "Incredibly ridiculous."

"But I'm still worried about you."

"Why?"

"Because Marc is...well...he's gorgeous," Barbara said, looking as if any woman who hadn't noticed was either a fool or half-blind. "He's so sexy. Not to mention the fact that he's kind, generous and trustworthy."

"Terrible qualities in a man, I know."

Barbara ignored that and continued on, "Don't get me wrong. He'd be perfect for you, someday, maybe.

But...it's just so soon, and I don't want to see you get hurt.''

"I'm not going to get hurt, because nothing's going on."

"But don't you see?" Barbara said. "He's perfect. And you're..."

"Poor, helpless Ginny, right? Can't take care of herself or her baby without Joe?"

She wasn't covering new ground here with Barbara. They were buddies, two unsuspecting women thrust into the midst of a big, nosy Italian family. They tended to stick together and to stick up for each other. So it hurt to find out that Barbara thought of her the way everyone else did.

"That's not what I meant at all," Barbara insisted. "It's just that Marc's a great guy. It would be easy to fall for him, but it's too soon."

"Too soon for what? Marc happened to be here last night, after his shift ended. Hannah got sick, and I panicked. He kept his head and helped me out when I was ready to fall apart. He slept in the recliner with Hannah, not with me."

"Okay," Barbara said, in a tone that indicated that it somehow wasn't okay.

Ginny counted to ten—it was something that she often did around the Reed family—then started again. "Say it with me this time. 'Nothing happened.'"

That managed to draw a wry smile out of Barbara. "I didn't say that anything happened."

Ginny drew a deep breath, much like the ones she'd learned in Lamaze. "He's a friend. That's all."

"Are you sure?"

Ginny hesitated, and that was her undoing. "I'm sure."

"You're also blushing."

* * *

Jimmy came by after work. Uncle Frank called. Mama
Reed left a message three times, and the last time Ginny
forced herself to speak with her mother-in-law.

Mama Reed had her own way of controlling her family. She assured Ginny that she believed her, that she knew
nothing had happened between Marc and her. She added
that she knew how much Ginny loved her Joey and that
Ginny would never do anything to disgrace his memory—with the emphasis placed heavily on the part where
Ginny would never do anything to disgrace Joe's memory.

Ginny got the message loud and clear. Guilty or not, it
looked bad. It had to stop, or there would be hell to pay.

When Marc called that night, she was ready. They
talked about Hannah. She told him how sorry she was
about that ugly scene with Jimmy and about whatever
he'd endured at work that day from any number of the
Reed clan, and then she got to the hard part.

"Are you still willing to help me?"

"Yes," he said.

"I don't want to cause trouble for you...."

"You let me worry about that, okay?"

"All right. But you'll have to be careful about coming
to the house—if you need to come to the house, I mean."

"I can do that."

"Lord," Ginny said, "then we'll really look guilty."

"If we get caught."

Ginny laughed in spite of herself. "You know, the
funny thing is, they all like you. And they swear that they
trust you."

"I'll keep that in mind in case I ever get the urge to
come courting one of the Reeds," he said wryly.

"Oh, no, I didn't even think of that. Are you seeing anyone right now, Marc?"

"No."

"Thank goodness. I'd hate to mess that up for you."

"There's nothing to mess up."

Ginny was relieved, but at the same time uneasy. She wondered why he was unattached, even as she decided she was glad he was. As Barbara had pointed out, Marc was a handsome man, a powerful one. Broad through the shoulder, narrow in the waist, he had an ease and a grace about himself that were seldom found in a man his age. He tamed his dark, curly hair by wearing it short. He had a wonderful smile and warm brown eyes.

She remembered his gentleness, his strength, when she had no business remembering those things. She'd drawn him into a hopeless mess by asking for his help, and yet his only concern had been for her.

Add to that the fact that he was wonderful with Hannah, and you had a very dangerous combination. The man had Daddy Material written all over him.

Of course, Ginny wasn't looking for a man at this point in her life—regardless of any daydreams she might have about Marc Dalton. Those little butterflies in the pit of her stomach must be stress. The heat that rose and spread from limb to limb when he took her hand in his must mean she was coming down with something Hannah had.

It was silly to think there was anything other than friendship between her and Marc.

"Ginny?" he said softly, sending a long, slow shiver down her spine and making her tense up all over again. "Try not to worry so much, okay?"

"I will."

"We'll give this a few days to blow over, and then we'll get back to work."

"All right."

"I'm pulling case files at the office on the investigations Joe and I had pending at the time of the shooting. If I don't find anything there, I'll want to go through his things. Are they still there?"

"In the walk-in closet, thrown into a dozen boxes or so."

"Good."

"What about—" she stumbled over the words, and had to force them out "—the...other woman?"

"I don't think there was another woman."

"I need to know, for sure."

"I can't find her if she doesn't exist."

"I know, but..."

"Let me think about that for a few days," Marc said. "I'll come up with something."

"Thanks."

"And, Ginny?"

"Yes."

"Kiss Hannah good-night for me."

Chapter 7

"There's nothing in the files," Marc told O'Connor a week later, as they sat in the coffee shop where they had met before. "Or if it's there, I can't find it. I still don't know what Joe was doing in front of that apartment building that day."

"We're running out of time," O'Connor said. "The trial's up next in Judge Miller's court. Whenever his current case ends, this one starts."

"And how long is that supposed to take?"

"Three weeks, maybe less, according to the prosecutor's best guess." O'Connor sipped his coffee. "What about Joey's home? Have you searched it yet?"

"You make me sound like a cat burglar," Marc protested, although maybe that was what he was. Maybe he was something even lower than that.

"You're a cop doing a job. Don't let your conscience keep you from doing your duty."

That didn't make Marc feel any better. "I have an open invitation from Joe's wife to go through the items collected from his desk at work and from his things still at the house."

"An invitation? I'm impressed."

Marc swore.

O'Connor pressed on. "What else have you got?"

"Probably nothing." Marc wouldn't have said anything at all if he didn't think the man was starting from the standpoint of wanting to prove Joe innocent. "Ginny has this ridiculous notion that he was having an affair before he died."

"Joey? He was crazy about that little girl."

"I know. I tried to tell her that."

"She have anything except suspicions?"

"Not really. But she thought Joe wasn't acting like himself."

"Still, it's a possibility. Morris's real troubles started when he slit his mistress's throat and came after her son."

"I know."

"The dead woman could have been friendly with Morris's partners, too."

"Too sleazy for Joe."

O'Connor shrugged. "He gets out on the streets, gets into something dirty, makes some new friends. It could have happened."

"I don't think so."

"Okay, do you have anything else yet?"

Again Marc dreaded saying it out loud. It seemed so damning. But O'Connor had to know. "Joe tried to get his wife out of town, right before he died. When she wouldn't go, he said he might need to get away. Said he needed to clear his head."

"And you still don't think he was cheating on her?"

"No. But I guess, as alternatives go, that one's not as bad as some of the others I've come up with."

O'Connor nodded. "He could have wanted his wife out of town because he thought she was in danger. He could have offended someone or scared someone who might be coming after him or who might try to get to Joe through that pretty wife of his."

Marc had already considered that himself. "There has to be another answer," Marc said.

"Find it," O'Connor demanded.

Find it, Marc thought. Sure. No problem. Go back to Ginny's. Tell a few more lies. Come even closer than he'd already come to kissing her. Fall even harder for that beautiful little girl of hers. And find some answers, while he was at it.

He waited until it was late, because the Reeds had finally calmed down about the night he'd spent at Ginny's and he didn't want to get them started again. He called first, then walked the four blocks to her house so that no one would see his car out front.

A week had gone by since his visit, and as much as he hated what had brought him back, he still looked forward to seeing Ginny. He was falling, harder and faster than ever before, and he didn't know what to do about it.

As Marc saw it, if he found the evidence that proved Joe was a crooked cop, he could forget about ever seeing Ginny again. She'd hate his guts. The family would stand guard twenty-four hours a day, if necessary, to keep him away—if they didn't just tear him limb from limb.

If Joe was innocent, if he could prove that, she might still hate him for his lack of faith in Joe and for the things he'd kept hidden from her.

He was boxed in. Either way he turned, he was in for trouble. But, as he saw it, it was too late to back out now.

He kept reminding himself that the job would be done, if not by him, then by someone who had no faith in Joe.

That person wouldn't be half in love with Ginny Reed, either. That person wouldn't be nearly as concerned with protecting her as he was.

He rationalized this all out with himself. And in the end it added up to him trying frantically to justify walking into her house one more time and lying to her. He tried to tell himself he was simply withholding information from her, but that wasn't right. As he saw it, what he was doing was nothing short of lying.

Ginny opened the door before he even knocked. Wearing a pair of faded jeans and a T-shirt, her hair piled casually on top of her head, she smiled at him and said, "Hi, stranger."

"Hi." He slipped past her, careful not to touch her, and told himself to keep his mind on the business at hand.

"I made coffee and a coffee cake, if you're hungry," Ginny said.

Which would mean going into the kitchen. He always seemed to get in trouble in the kitchen. "Maybe later?"

"Sure."

"So, are you under surveillance? Or has the commotion died down by now?"

Ginny shrugged. "I'm still getting a lot of phone calls, and a suspicious number of early-morning visitors. You were smart to walk over tonight."

"I'm really sorry about that. I just never thought they'd react that way."

"Don't you dare apologize. You were just trying to help. And if it helps, the votes are all in. They've given you the family stamp of approval now. You're free to date the Reed cousin of your choice."

"Just not you?"

She nodded.

Marc wondered if she thought it was such an outlandish idea—the thought of being involved with him. But he would not let himself take this conversation one step further. "So, did I miss Hannah?"

"She's asleep, hopefully until at least four in the morning."

"Ouch. What a rude awakening."

"Oh, you can't imagine. She wakes up starving and howling like a banshee. Imagine something about ten times worse than any alarm clock you've ever owned."

"And she goes off every morning at 4:00 a.m.?"

"If I'm lucky, she waits that long."

"Ginny, you mean to tell me you haven't slept through the night in almost four months?"

"More than that. Nobody sleeps through the night when they're eight or nine months pregnant."

"You should be a zombie by now. How in the world do you do it?"

"Loving her more than anything in this world helps a little," Ginny said. "It doesn't hurt that she's adorable, either."

"She is that."

"Don't think she doesn't know it, either. We had pictures taken this week, and you should have seen her playing to the camera. I swear, sometimes I think she's eighteen years old."

"I missed her," Marc said, unable to help himself.

"You could risk sneaking in the back door in broad daylight, if you wanted."

"I may have to do that."

And then they just stood there in the hallway, not saying anything for a moment, Ginny's gaze locked on his. She looked away first. "I guess we should get started."

"Sure."

"Come on upstairs. I pulled everything into the bedroom closet, but I didn't want to take it downstairs, not with all these people dropping by unexpectedly."

She led the way. Marc followed as she stopped in what he was sure was the master bedroom, one that looked as if it had hardly been touched in months. Or maybe even a year? Marc looked at Ginny questioningly.

"I moved into the guest room after Joe died."

"Oh." He didn't want to be in the bedroom she and Joe had shared.

"Everything in the boxes either came from his desk at work or from different parts of the house. And I haven't moved any of his things from the bedroom or this closet yet."

"Okay. Did you go through these things at all?"

She shook her head. "But I could help you now. It would make things go faster, and...from what I hear, we don't have much time."

"Doesn't look like it. We're up next in Judge Miller's court."

"I know. The TV stations and the newspapers have started calling already."

"Get the number changed. Or let me take care of it. I have a friend at the phone company. He'll get it done tomorrow."

"I . . . Okay."

"Hey." The back of his hand was under her chin, bringing her face up to his, before he knew what he'd done. The connection was quick, the feeling heady and dangerous, just from touching her chin. "I'm not trying to imply that you can't do this on your own. I'm saying I have connections that can get it done quicker. And I don't mind helping. Ginny, let me help."

She stepped back right away and took a breath. He watched the rise and fall of her breasts, all the while telling himself not to.

"All right," she said. "But I don't want to cause trouble for you, Marc. I know what Jimmy and the rest of them can be like. I feel bad enough about what's happened already."

"I'm not afraid of a little trouble," he said. Everything he felt for her frightened him, but trouble with the Reed family didn't.

"Okay."

"Now, where do we start? Do you know where the office things are?"

"There." She pointed to two boxes on the floor, below a row of suits.

Marc hauled them out of the closet and set them on the floor, still avoiding the bed at all costs. He picked a corner and sat on the carpet. "I think I'll need to spread out," he said.

"I'll take this one. What am I looking for?"

"Well, I'm anxious to find Joe's notebooks. He always kept a little one that would fit in his back pocket, where he wrote down names and phone numbers. He jotted down ideas about cases we were working on, theories, unanswered questions. Most cops have one."

"I know the one you're talking about. He had it with him all the time."

"Right. I don't remember seeing his when I cleaned out his desk, but that's not unusual. He probably had it on him, or in the car." Marc had talked his way into a corner before he realized what he'd done.

"Where else could it be?" Ginny said innocently.

Marc looked away, wondering just how much pain was waiting for her as they went through this process of finding out what happened to her husband. They seemed to hit new trouble spots every day.

"Ginny, if he had it on him, you should have gotten it when his personal effects came back."

She paled as understanding dawned. "From the morgue."

"Yeah. Sorry."

"It's all right. I told you, I knew going in that this wasn't going to be any picnic."

"You can still change your mind."

"No, I can't," she said.

Then they would keep going. "Do you remember getting anything back from the morgue?"

"No, but I'm not sure if I would have remembered, or if anyone would have told me. Someone in the family probably picked up the package and tucked it away somewhere without mentioning it."

Marc thought about that. "Do you have his wallet? Or his wedding ring? Those should have been part of the package."

"I know I got the ring back." She turned and pulled open a drawer, coming up with the plain gold band that had been wrapped around her husband's finger for ten years. "You didn't tell me. Did you find out anything about...another woman?"

"No, nothing. I asked a few people I thought I could trust not to go running to one of the Reeds. They all looked at me like I was crazy."

"Still, if he was doing something like that, he wouldn't exactly take out an ad in the paper."

"The man was absolutely, positively, in love with you. I can't believe..." Marc had planned to tell her that he didn't understand how she couldn't see that. But then, he'd always managed to keep his feelings for her a secret. At least he hoped they were still a secret.

"What can't you believe?"

He swallowed hard and looked away. "That you couldn't see how he felt. That you didn't feel it yourself."

Ginny didn't say anything. Marc didn't want to say anything else. He settled for adding, "Why don't we dig into these boxes and see if we can find something here?"

Two hours later, they still hadn't found Joe's most recent notebook. The others, little red spiral ones sized to fit into a pocket, were stacked neatly in a locked box in the top of the closet. They were all dated, the last one breaking off three months before Joe had been shot. Marc took the whole box, hoping that whatever was bothering Joe had started more than three months prior to his death.

"We still need the last one," Marc said.

"It has to be here." Puzzled, Ginny looked around the room, which was strewn with stacks of papers.

"We'll just have to find it. If this problem of Joe's was police business, something in that book will tell us what it was."

"So what are you going to do?"

Marc thought for a moment. "I'll start with the funeral director and see if he remembers turning over Joe's personal effects to someone. That way, you won't have to start questioning the whole family yet."

"Joe's family's going to go ballistic over this," she said. "Just the idea that I want to know. And then, by going to you, rather than keeping this inside the family..."

Of course, she didn't know the half of it. The family would do worse than go ballistic when everything came out. And he was going to be right in the line of fire.

"What else do we need to do?" Ginny asked.

"You don't remember anything he said? Any names, any dates, any cases at all? Anything to indicate what case he might have been worrying over?"

She shook her head.

"Just keep trying. Something may come back to you." Marc looked around at the papers, the empty boxes, the drawers, the neatly folded piles of clothes. "His clothes are still hanging in that closet?"

Ginny glanced at the open door of the walk-in closet. "Yes."

"Go through the pockets of all his shirts, his jackets and his pants. Go through the drawers, and everything in them."

"Okay."

"Did he have any kind of special hiding place around the house? Any kind of safe?"

"No, but . . . I guess I need to think about getting one, because I still have Joe's revolver in a box somewhere and I'd feel safer, with Hannah, if the gun was locked up."

Marc didn't like the sound of that at all. "Are you sure you want the revolver in the house?"

Ginny hesitated. "I don't know."

"Do you know how to shoot it?"

"Yes." But she didn't sound that sure of herself.

"How long has it been since you shot a gun?"

Ginny shrugged. "A couple of years, at least."

"You'd be better off with a baseball bat under your bed."

"You have a gun."

"I know my way around a gun. You don't."

She didn't say anything for a moment.

"Look," he said, "if you want to keep the revolver, I'll help you get up to speed with it. But if you keep it, you have to be prepared to use it. You don't want to be figuring out whether you have the stomach for shooting someone while you have the gun in your hand and you're staring down someone who's just broken into your house. That's when the intruder panics and shoots you first."

"Oh."

"Do you think you'd be able to shoot someone?"

"I think so, if I thought Hannah was in danger."

Marc wasn't so sure. "For now, I'll bring you a baseball bat."

Ginny smiled. "Okay. And I'll think about the gun."

"Meanwhile, lock it up, even if Hannah isn't even crawling. You still have all her cousins running through this place from time to time, and you can't be too careful with a gun."

She gave him a smile and a look that said she was trying to hold her tongue.

"Okay, so maybe you just bring out this rabid protective streak in people."

Ginny smiled. "Maybe."

"Lock up the gun," he said again, unable to help himself. "And think about Joe's hiding places, too. The notebook's so small, he could have stashed it anywhere. I'll come back tomorrow night and help you look for it."

"Oh." She glanced at the clock, which showed it was almost midnight. "I didn't realize it was so late. You need to get home so you can get to work in the morning."

He nodded and grabbed the closest box, ready to stack them back in the closet. "And you need to get some sleep. Four a.m. comes awfully early."

"Just leave the boxes," Ginny said. "You've done enough for one night. I can straighten up tomorrow."

"All right."

They headed downstairs, and he caught himself as he turned toward the front door. "I forgot we're working on a clandestine operation here." He turned and headed for the kitchen door.

Glancing at the lock made him think of one more thing. "Ginny, did you ever get Joe's keys back?"

She hesitated. "I'm not sure. I had my own set for everything, so I never really thought about it."

"Think about it. If you don't have those keys, someone has a way to get into your house."

"I remember now," she said. "Somebody brought Joe's truck home—Christopher, or one of the other cousins. I don't remember which one. But the keys must be around here somewhere."

"Wait a minute. This is your house you're talking about. *Someone* doesn't cut it. Find out who and get those keys back. Remember, whoever has them could just walk right in."

"We're talking about family here." She started to argue, then held up her hands in surrender when she saw the look on his face. "I'll find out who has the keys."

"First thing in the morning," he insisted. "Either that or get the locks changed."

"Oh, come on, Marc."

"Your house," he reminded her. "And you don't have any idea where those keys are now or who's had access to them in all the time they've been missing."

"Okay, I'll take care of it."

"Tomorrow?"

"I promise. Tomorrow. Now, do you think you'll be able to sleep tonight?"

"Not as well as I would knowing those locks were changed."

She laughed then. He had the door open, was halfway outside, when Ginny caught him with a hand in the crook of his arm. He looked down at her delicate fingers, curled around his biceps. Her touch was light; the effect was not.

"I really appreciate everything you're doing to help," she said.

And then the whole world around them faded away. Marc saw her face coming closer, saw her lashes flutter down, saw her lips pressed together, no doubt headed for a chaste kiss against his cheek.

Everything inside him slowed down to this surreal speed. He saw the whole thing so clearly, yet at the same time it had this dreamlike quality to it.

He knew that light, sweet fragrance that hung in the air around her, knew the sound of her voice and the way it had of skimming over his skin and setting his nerve endings on edge, knew how narrow her shoulders and her waist were, because of the times he'd held her in his arms in an honest effort to do no more than comfort her.

Her lips came closer still, no doubt intent on brushing softly against his face with the touch of one friend to another, but he was long past that.

Marc moved faster than he would have thought possible. Her lips did indeed brush against his cheek, and in the next instant he caught her by the arms and pulled her closer, until her body was flush against his. With one hand, he gave a little tug on her hair, just enough to tilt her head back a fraction of an inch, so that his lips could find hers.

She gasped in surprise, but she didn't pull away. Her lips parted on the slight sound she made, and he took full advantage of that. He covered her mouth with his and savored the taste of her, the textures of her, the feel of her.

His heart, after skipping two full beats, took off like a freight train, and all his senses came alive.

He kissed her once, twice, then again, wishing he could make this moment last forever, knowing he would pay dearly for it, but unable to hold back any longer. Having her this close was simply too great a temptation for him to endure.

Her mouth trembled beneath his. Her hands held on tight to his shoulders, not pulling him closer, but not pushing him away, either. The taste of her was sweeter than anything he'd ever imagined, and he wanted to devour her with his mouth.

He brought his hand up to her face, to her cheek, tilting her head to the left to give him better access, and he kissed her like the desperate, starving man he was. He kissed her for what seemed an eternity, until the whole world started slowing down again and the roaring in his ears receded. Finally, he knew it was true; he was actually holding this woman in his arms. This wasn't the dream of a desperate man, but reality. Sweet, hot, sinful reality.

For the longest time, he would have sworn this day would never come. He had his tongue inside her mouth, stroking hers, slowly now, savoring the feeling of being inside her in this small yet intimate way. His heart was pounding, so hard it drowned out everything else. His body was hot and hard, aching for her, and he had to pull away before she figured out just how close he was to losing control.

Still he lingered over her mouth, stroking, tasting, savoring, aching now.

Ginny. He meant to stop. He knew he was living on borrowed time. *Please,* the voice inside him begged. *Don't let it end. Not yet. Not now. Not ever.*

Her lips yielded to his, her hands still clutching at his shoulders. She was breathing as hard as he was, and when she sagged into him he held her even tighter.

He stroked her lips with his tongue now, the frenzy giving way to a deep, languorous heat.

She turned her head slightly to the side, and he turned with her, kissing her again, fearing that this was it, the only time he'd ever get to do this. And he didn't want it to end.

"Aw, Ginny," he said, when he managed to pull away enough to speak. For a second, he let his forehead rest there against hers. Backing up another fraction, he saw the flush of heat in her cheeks, saw her trembling lower lip, saw her eyes questioning his for an instant before she glanced away.

She stepped back, clasped her hands together in front of her, no doubt ready to push him away if he tried that again. She wouldn't look at him.

"I'm sorry." It was the only thing he could say. Then he turned and walked away, before he made things any worse.

Chapter 8

Ginny watched as Marc walked out the door and down the alley without looking back. She shut the door, locked it with a trembling hand, then stood there in her kitchen—hers and Joe's—and felt like a traitor. And a fool.

She didn't think anyone had ever kissed her like that. Of its own volition, her hand came up to her mouth, and her fingers rested momentarily against her trembling lips.

Ginny didn't have a great deal of experience with men. She'd gone into Joe's arms in high school, married him at eighteen and lived with him for the rest of his life.

That had been eleven years ago, and these were the nineties, she reasoned with herself. Maybe men kissed other women like that these days and it didn't mean a thing.

Well, it meant something to her. She wasn't sure what, but it definitely meant something.

Her whole body had come to life under the power of that kiss. Her knees had nearly buckled. Her heart had kicked into overdrive, and if she hadn't been hanging on to him, she would have fallen to the floor.

And she wasn't sure she would have stopped him if he hadn't pulled away on his own. She'd been too surprised at first. Then too intrigued by the whole situation.

She'd come alive again in Marc's arms.

"Oh, my God," she said, turning around and sliding down to the floor. Her knees bent, she laid her head against them, put her hands over her head, trying to block out everything else.

It was just a kiss, she tried telling herself, but she wasn't that good a liar.

She tried reasoning with herself again, this time admitting up front that he was a very attractive man. It was only natural that she would feel *something* if he kissed her.

Ginny sighed. Who was she trying to kid? *Something* was a totally inadequate word to describe Marc's kiss.

Firecrackers? Shooting stars? Walls tumbling down? That was more like it. Had anyone ever kissed her and brought the walls tumbling down?

She felt like a traitor just for allowing herself to think of that question. She had loved her husband, despite their problems. If anyone had asked, she would have said the physical side of their relationship was fine.

Fine, not firecrackers. But then, they'd been married for ten years. Who got firecrackers after ten years?

Ginny closed her eyes, wishing she could block out her own thoughts as easily. But she couldn't.

Marc?

It was so hard to believe.

Marc had kissed her like . . . like he couldn't get enough of her, couldn't get close enough, couldn't make himself let go.

She wondered if he kissed every woman like that, wondered what had possessed him to do so and what he must think of her for responding to him that way.

She wondered how she would ever face him again. Her head sank even lower at that thought. What would she say to him? How would she explain?

It was silly, but she felt the same way she had after she'd kissed Joe for the first time. She'd been so naive, so shy and reserved, that none of the boys at school paid any attention to her, until Joe came along.

This was like starting all over again, except she had no idea what she and Marc had started or even if they'd started *anything*.

"This is crazy," she said to herself. "Crazy."

And then she went upstairs, where she tossed and turned until Hannah woke up and demanded to be fed.

Ginny would have sworn that nothing could make her seek out Marc's company the next day, but a mysterious phone call proved her undoing.

Shaken, angry and confused, she made her way to the precinct house, a place she hadn't entered since months before Joe died. Once there, she started searching for Marc. The desk sergeant, a man she'd known for years, pumped her hand, gave her a big smile, then directed her to the same corner of the office where Joe and Marc used to sit.

Walking quickly and quietly, careful not to make eye contact with anyone, Ginny made her way through the crowded office. She tried not to think about the familiar sound of the phones ringing, the hum of conversation, the static from the police radio in the corner.

Still, she couldn't help but notice the way activity seemed to come to a halt as she passed through the room and people recognized her. A few of them called her name. She looked up and gave them a tight smile. Finally she halted in the middle of the room and turned to an officer whose name escaped her at the moment.

"I'm looking for Marc Dalton," she said. "Do you know where I can find him?"

"Sure do, Mrs. Reed," the officer said, then motioned for her to follow him.

They threaded their way through a sea of desks until they came to the back of the room, where the officer knocked on a closed door, then opened it.

"You have a visitor," the officer said.

Before Ginny had a moment to prepare herself, she was face-to-face with Marc. She watched as his body tensed, his chin came up a fraction and his eyes narrowed. For a moment, he seemed to be speechless, then incredulous at the idea that she was standing before him.

"I need to talk to you," she said.

He hesitated a moment, then seemed almost uncertain. Funny, she didn't remember ever associating a thing like uncertainty with him before. Finally he motioned her inside and shut the door behind her. "You want to do this here? Now?"

Ginny looked away. Immediately she felt heat flood her cheeks. Not twelve hours ago, she'd been in his arms, her body plastered against his, her arms clutching at his shoulders, her legs threatening to give way beneath her. She stopped to take a breath, as the sensations hit her with a fierceness that had her thinking it might have been half a second ago, instead of half a day.

Swallowing hard, she told herself she couldn't think about that desperate kiss now. She had to stay focused.

"Not that," she said, intending to force herself to laugh. It came out as more of a choking sound. "I don't think we need to talk about that at all, not ever."

"Ever?"

He seemed to have a hard time accepting her answer. She didn't care. "I need to talk about Joe."

Ginny had thought long and hard before coming. Twelve days ago, she'd made the very difficult decision to put her trust in Marc. She'd already done the hardest part. She'd confided in him about her fears that Joe was about to leave her, and she didn't think she could bring herself to share that secret with anyone else. If she gave up on Marc now, because of the kiss, where would she turn for help?

"Are you still willing to help me?" she asked.

"Of course I am."

Ginny nodded. "Good, because someone just called me and told me that a bullet my husband fired the day he was killed nearly hit an FBI agent, and I—I need to know if that's true."

Marc stared at her, as if he were trying to figure out how much to tell her.

"Tell me everything," she insisted. "I know that look. Joe's family gives it to me all the time, and I'm tired of it. I'm not going to accept it anymore. When I came to you for help, I did so because I hoped you wouldn't treat me the way they do."

At first, Marc said nothing.

Ginny pleaded her case. "Don't let me down now, Marc. Tell me what you know about this."

"All right. Sit down."

He held out a chair. Grateful to get off her feet, Ginny sank into it. "Did Joe nearly kill an agent that day?"

"I don't know about nearly killing him, but we dug a bullet fired from his revolver out of the wall of a building at the scene, and an FBI agent swears it whizzed right past his head."

Ginny could have crumpled to the floor right then. She'd thought he might deny it. She hoped desperately that it wasn't true, even now, as she struggled to figure out what it meant.

Think like a cop, she told herself. She'd lived with one long enough to know how to do that. What were the questions that mattered? What were the possibilities?

"*Did* Joe fire that shot?"

"There was only one shot fired from his gun, and he had gunpowder residue on his hands."

"Why? Why would he shoot at an agent?"

"Ginny, the scene just exploded. It happens sometimes. You get a lot of uptight people in a small area with guns. The first shot's fired, and that's it. Everybody starts firing. And you couldn't tell the crooks from the cops that day, because one of the crooks *was* a cop."

She tried to accept that, and failed. "Joe wasn't a reckless cop. He wouldn't have fired if there was any doubt in his mind about who he would hit."

"It doesn't always work like that," Marc insisted. "He would have had seconds. Hesitating, even for a fraction of a second, can get you killed on the streets. Joe knew that."

Ginny wasn't convinced. "What aren't you telling me?"

"Who told you about the bullet?"

"I don't know who it was. He wouldn't tell me his name." Ginny refused to let him change the subject. "Your turn. What else aren't you telling me?"

"Ginny, could we talk about this later, maybe when we're not in the middle of the precinct house and half a dozen cops aren't watching us?"

"You're stalling," she told him.

"Do you want to explain this scene to Mama Reed and the rest of the crew? Because that's where we're headed here. You know someone's going to take this back to the family."

Ginny wanted to curse. She did, but under her breath. Force of habit had her trying not to say naughty words out loud where Hannah might hear, and now she did that automatically.

She was so mad. And scared. And hurt. "You knew about the bullet," she said accusingly. "What else do you know that you haven't told me?"

"Ginny..." he said, nodding toward the glass door.

She glanced that way, saw people staring, then quickly looking away. They knew what this was about, and she didn't.

"He was my husband," she said. "And you were supposed to be his friend. You were supposed to be my friend, too."

"I am," he replied, his jaw tense.

Seeing him like this, at the precinct house, on the job, reminded her that there was steel in this man now that hadn't been there ten years ago. There was determination and guts and an inner strength she'd always admired, and now there was more. Mama Reed said he was grounded, that his foundation was solid.

Ginny felt as if she'd just been thrown up against a brick wall, when she'd expected to find some comfort, some reassurance, some answers. She'd always felt so at ease with Marc, and somehow that had disappeared, as well, in less than a day. Suddenly she just wanted to escape. "I have to go."

He caught her by the arm, his fingers curling around her forearm in a touch that was as unsettling as it was brief. "I'll come by tonight, after I'm done here. Wait for me," he instructed, "before you go to anyone else and start asking questions."

She didn't answer him, just looked at him for a moment. Then she left, all the while wondering, if she couldn't trust in Marc, who could she trust?

Marc didn't understand how everything had gone so wrong in so short a time. As he walked down the alley, part of the path that connected Ginny's house to his, he shook his head and tried to make sense of the situation.

Everything had been . . . okay, until last night. One little thing, like her lips coming toward him, had simply shortcircuited every defense he'd built up against the woman. Before he knew what hit him, he'd had her in his arms. He'd felt her mouth beneath his, her breath mingling with his, her body locked against his, and his senses had been sent reeling.

Even now, remembering every texture, every sigh, every curve of her sweet, delicate body, he had trouble believing the whole scene had been real.

How could he have kissed Ginny that way?

How was he ever going to forget it?

How would he ever make her understand, when he couldn't begin to understand himself?

It was impossible. The two of them together was impossible. Too much guilt. Too many memories.

Marc shook his head. He had to quit dreaming, had to think and react like a cop on a mission and not a man who simply ached for a woman he couldn't have.

Someone had called her. Someone was trying to stir up trouble. Who would do that? And why? What did anyone have to gain by causing trouble for Ginny? By getting her nervous and making her doubt her own husband?

Morris, that was who.

Marc swore as he reached the back door. The answer was so obvious. Morris definitely had reason to want her nervous and doubting Joe. So, what would the man's next move be? And exactly how did he plan to take advantage of Ginny's uneasiness?

Marc had to analyze the situation, to plan, to anticipate the man's next move, if he was going to win this battle.

He glanced up at Ginny's house. Lights shone through the blinds downstairs. Flowers bloomed in the clay pots on the back steps and in the flower beds alongside the house and the walkways. Trees spread their branches overhead, embracing the house and filtering out the moonlight and the glow from the streetlights out front.

It seemed so peaceful, so normal, yet nothing was normal about this. Marc feared that what little peace might exist inside the walls of this house was about to be destroyed, unless he managed to pull off a miracle.

Ginny Reed needed a miracle. He intended to find her one. Grim but determined, he knocked on the back door and waited. Ginny was there in seconds, which told him she must have been watching for him. He walked inside, then glanced down at her, taking in her casual jeans and knit top, her hair, pulled back into a mass of curls at the back of her neck, the lack of any makeup or jewelry, the flash of color burning in her cheeks.

She looked him in the eye for just a moment, then fastened the chain on the door before turning to stand in front of it.

"I wasn't sure you'd come," she said.

"I wasn't sure I should." *Because I wanted to kiss you, again.*

He'd wager that wasn't what was on her mind, but he couldn't help himself. Now that he'd kissed her for real, he couldn't stop dreaming about doing it again.

Marc watched as faint color flooded her face and her lashes swept down across cheeks so soft that the idea of touching them took his breath away.

"Come in and sit down," Ginny said, walking into the living room.

He followed, surprised to find Hannah awake and smiling at him from her spot in the corner, on the floor. She held out her hand to him, and her whole face lit up. Marc felt as if someone had taken the weight of the world off his shoulders. He went to Hannah and scooped her up from her seat.

"Well, hello, little one," he whispered in her ear, as she laid her head on his shoulder and started gnawing on the collar of his jacket. "It's a good thing she doesn't have teeth."

Ginny, her expression guarded, held out her hands for the baby. "I'll take her."

Marc wasn't ready to give her up. "I don't mind. I'll keep her." To Hannah he whispered, "Hello, little lady," as she slobbered on his favorite shirt.

Ginny stood there watching him with the baby, and the look on her face told him that she was quite uncomfortable.

Marc decided to see how long they could stick to safe topics. "What's she doing up at this hour? She's not sick again, is she?"

"No, she's fine. She just hasn't quite mastered the art of telling time yet."

"I'm glad," Marc said, and it wasn't just for the reprieve before dealing with the issues at hand. "I missed her."

"Oh, Marc." Ginny sounded tired, and a little desperate.

"What?" he asked. "Do you look at me with her and think about how much she's missing with Joe gone?"

"That's part of it," she said, but there was clearly much more than that.

Marc didn't care for the direction his own thoughts were taking. Did she wonder about finding a man who'd grow to be Hannah's father someday? Was she picturing another man here? Holding her daughter this way? Loving this wonderful baby smell of hers? Smiling while she gnawed on his collar?

He felt a snarl work its way across his face at the thought of Ginny and another man.

Marc hadn't been able to get that idea out of his head ever since the day of Hannah's baptism. She would find another man.

So why not me? He could torment himself by thinking of kissing her again, so he might as well tackle the really difficult things like that. If Ginny was going to find another man someday...

Why not me?

Why not indeed?

His heart going ninety miles an hour, he let that thought rattle around inside his head.

So many times, he'd told himself it was impossible. He'd loved her husband like a brother, and now he was trying to figure out if Joe had been a dirty cop. He was lying to Joe's wife, listening to her deepest, darkest secrets, cradling Joe's baby in his arms and kissing Ginny in Joe's kitchen.

And those things were just the reasons he could come up with off the top of his head. Given some time, he was sure he could find more.

But he wasn't going to leave it at that. The impossible wasn't enough to hold him back now. He was going to find a way to make it happen.

"I don't know what to say to you," he said, at a total loss. "I know I owe you an explanation for what I did last night, but you're not going to like it. And it's probably going to complicate matters even more."

"You don't have to explain," Ginny insisted.

"Oh, I think I do," he said, feeling a little reckless right now, desperate and drunk on the irrational hope that he might someday be the man she chose for herself and her daughter. "I think it's go-for-broke time. It's pretty obvious what's going on anyway."

"Is it?"

Was she bluffing? Or had she honestly not figured it out? Whatever the answer, Marc didn't see any need to hide his feelings. He didn't think he could. And if she did start searching for another man someday, he intended to be the first in line.

He leaned his cheek against the top of Hannah's head, now pressed against his shoulder. Suddenly everything seemed so clear. The fog had lifted. The path he was meant to take lay spread out before him, like an invitation he couldn't resist.

He wanted Ginny. He wanted Hannah. He wanted everything Joe had left behind, even if the guilt of stepping into his friend's shoes might someday eat him alive.

After all, Joe was gone. Ginny and Hannah were alone now.

Yes, Marc decided, the time for pussyfooting around was long past.

"Ginny," he began, "I want you to know that I never meant for this to happen."

Ginny watched the play of emotions flicker across his face, and something she saw there frightened her. He'd seemed almost bleak at first, then resigned, then... She could only think of the sensation that he'd been reborn right in front of her eyes. She saw the determination she associated so clearly with him now, the fierceness, the unshakable resolve.

He had a plan, and she didn't think she was going to like it.

She backed away, one step, then two, until she found her back against the wall. She didn't want to know what Marc had to say. "No," she managed to get out.

Seeing Marc this way, the way he held Hannah so tenderly, the obvious affection between them, reminded her of being held in those same arms. She knew what it was like to be cradled against that powerful chest, to lean on those broad shoulders of his. And after last night, she knew other things as well about being in his arms.

"No," she said again, wondering how she'd failed to see this coming, wondering how awkward things could possibly become between them.

"Sorry, sweetheart," he said with a familiar twinkle in his eyes. "The answer is yes. I'm afraid I'm crazy about you. I think I have been since I moved back to town twelve years ago, right after you got engaged to Joe."

"Oh, no." She closed her eyes and looked away. The strength just seemed to evaporate inside her body, leaving her a mass of boneless, formless, trembling woman.

Crazy about you.

The words echoed around inside her head, which had emptied of everything else and left all her attention, all her senses, focused on Marc.

He was different tonight, she decided. Or maybe she was seeing him differently now. Maybe she was seeing him clearly for the first time in a long time. For so long, he'd been just a boy she knew. And then he'd been Joe's friend and partner, accepted as a de facto member of the family, as welcome in her kitchen in the morning for a cup of coffee as any of the brothers or the cousins who were constantly dropping by.

While she wasn't paying attention, he'd turned into a man. A very attractive and compelling man, a force to be reckoned with.

Crazy about you. "Oh, no."

"I fought it," he continued. "I've been fighting for years, and I'm sorry I made you uncomfortable last night. Sorry I pounced on you like that. I hope I didn't frighten you."

She shook her head. *Frightened* wasn't the word she would have used, not exactly. She couldn't think right now just what the one-word description of what he'd done to her last night in the kitchen might be. She didn't think she could put it into a hundred words, for that matter.

But she wished he hadn't told her any of these things. She tried to wish he hadn't kissed her, but that seemed beyond her. She did wish he didn't look so perfect holding her daughter.

It's impossible, she told herself, and then in the same breath, started imagining ways it might be possible after all.

She knew Marc. She trusted him. He was a good man, a kind, generous, loving one. Before last night, she would have said she'd be safe with him, but she certainly hadn't felt safe in his arms.

She'd felt the thrill of danger, of the forbidden, the unknown, but it had been much more than that. Even she wasn't that naive. She'd realized, once she stopped trying to lie to herself, that she could go outside tonight and kiss the first dozen men she saw and not begin to feel the way she'd felt kissing Marc.

"I don't know what to say," she managed at last.

He shook his head and dared to smile. He really was gorgeous when he smiled. And she could have fantasies for days about those shoulders of his.

"You don't have to say anything. You don't have to do anything. I just didn't see the point in trying to hide my feelings from you any longer."

Ginny swallowed hard and wondered what her next move should be. What did a woman do with a man who confessed to being crazy about her?

"I'm still going to be your friend," he said. "I'll still help you find out about Joe."

"Joe..." The guilt nearly swamped her.

"Wait a minute," he said, reading her all too easily. "Joe is gone. I miss him, Ginny. I loved him, too. But he's gone. Don't go feeling guilty because the whole time you were with him I was daydreaming about you and me."

"I can't do that."

"No, listen to me. You didn't do anything wrong."

"It feels wrong," she said. Surely he had to feel that, as well. "It feels like cheating on Joe."

"I know, sweetheart. Believe me, I know."

Ginny fidgeted with the buttons on her sweater and tried to look anywhere but at him. "I can't handle this."

"There's nothing to handle," he said. "I told you, nothing has to change between us. I've felt this way for a long time and managed to keep my hands off you. I can do it again. I think."

Ginny's gaze locked on his. She heard the teasing quality of his voice, saw the twinkle in his eyes, the dimple in his cheek when he grinned. Hannah nestled against him, as if to tell Ginny she'd made her choice and she was quite happy with it.

And he was crazy about her.

Now why should that knowledge flow through her like three glasses of champagne, heading straight for her head and making her dizzy and warm all over? Why should that make her want to kiss him again? Why should that make her fingers itch to wrap themselves around those glorious muscles in his upper arms and hang on for dear life while he set her senses on fire again?

"Don't look at me like that, Ginny Reed," he warned.

She felt the shame well up in her heart, warring with the desire. She wasn't sure which one of those would have won, wasn't sure whether she would have managed to resist him or not. And she didn't get the chance to find out.

This time she saw it coming a mile away. He took three strides across the room. With one arm wrapped protectively around Hannah, he came to her. His other arm turned her more fully toward him, then landed at the base of her neck. His gaze lost its teasing quality and turned deadly serious.

Her heart leaped inside her chest. Her hands came up and splayed against the wall of his chest, feeling the heat of him, and the power.

"Damn," he muttered. "And I told myself I wasn't going to kiss you again."

She thought for a moment that he wasn't, and she would have been greatly disappointed if he hadn't. But in the next instant his lips, smooth and insistent, closed over hers. The breath abandoned her lungs, leaving on a sigh that had her parting her lips beneath his. She could have sworn he was smiling as he kissed her.

The power, the electricity, was still there, just as strong as before. It hit like a bolt of lightning, piercing her heart and leaving her wide open and vulnerable as never before.

She remembered the way it had been the night before, the sensation of being swept away.

She wanted to kiss him some more, to see where else he would take her, what things he could show her that she'd never seen before.

Between them, Hannah wriggled and squirmed. When that didn't work, she whined, then roared with that baby-lion sound she favored so much.

"Oh!" Ginny jumped back.

Marc took his time about pulling away, the satisfaction on his face plain for her to see.

Ginny touched her fingertips to her lips, which still quivered and quaked in the wake of his touch. What had he done to her? How had he managed in an instant to turn her whole world upside down? And what in the world was she going to do about this... attraction he professed to have for her?

She had no idea. Absolutely no clue. She just shook her head, all reason, all logic, deserting her.

"Sorry," he said, almost managing to sound sincerely apologetic about the fact that they'd been locked in each other's arms only moments before. "That's the way it is."

Chapter 9

Twenty-four hours later, Ginny still had no answers for what Marc's confession meant to her. She remembered the kiss, the glint of satisfaction in his eyes when he'd pulled away from her, the determination in his voice when he'd staked his claim, telling her, "That's the way it is."

Which prompted her to ask herself what she was going to do about his feelings for her. Which in turn had her wondering what she wanted from him. Which made her blush.

Ginny was a mass of nerves and confusion, and her sister-in-law knew it.

Ginny and Hannah had joined the Reed clan for dinner at Barbara and Jimmy's house, after their oldest son's first Little League championship-winning game. Barbara kept cornering her in the big, comfortable kitchen, trying to drag the whole story out of Ginny.

Having taken more than her share of nosy questions about Marc already—and this time having something to feel guilty about—Ginny was in no shape to face Barbara, who knew her too well.

"You don't turn three different shades of pink over nothing," Barbara said finally, as she and Ginny shared cleanup duty. "Spill it, before I go get Mama Reed and let her drag it out of you."

"I told you. I told everybody. Nothing happened." Damned if she didn't blush over that half-truth once again.

Still, it was just a kiss. Okay, a couple of kisses. Great kisses.

"Ginny," Barbara said in warning.

"Barbara. I've known him since before I bought my first training bra."

"So, you'd known Joe that long, too."

Just then, the back door opened and shut with a bang. Jimmy made his way through the kitchen, followed by Christopher and Antonio, arguing the merits of one of the umpire's calls. Ginny waited until the room cleared and searched for a reason to turn the conversation to something else. Finally, she found an opening.

"So, what happened to Antonio's bride-to-be? I don't think she's missed a family gathering in years. What gives?"

"I don't know, I don't care, and I'm not going to let you change the subject on me. It won't work. We were talking about you and you-know-who."

"No, you're talking. I'm not. I'm done. I'm taking my daughter and going home."

Barbara followed her throughout the house as she collected Hannah from Mama Reed, collected Hannah's diaper bag, which had become a de facto purse for Ginny, and turned down no fewer than three offers of rides home from the overprotective men of the Reed clan.

"Please don't be mad at me," Barbara said when Ginny was loading Hannah into her car seat.

Ginny managed to smile as she turned to Barbara and gave her a hug. "I'm just all out of sorts, okay? I think...it's the trial. It's made me edgy."

"You're sure?"

Ginny went back and forth between her desire to talk and her utter confusion over what she might say. Finally, she told Barbara, "I guess you were right. He's too perfect."

"Too tempting?"

Ginny nodded.

"Too gorgeous?"

"Yes."

"Too sexy?"

"Barbara, you're not helping."

"Sorry."

"It would be too easy to fall for him."

Barbara gave her one of her concerned-mother looks. "Be careful. I don't want to see you get hurt."

"Marc would never hurt me."

"But the relationship could."

"I know." The family's reaction was all too predictable, no matter how high their regard for Marc. "I really have to go. It's past Hannah's bedtime."

"Sure. Call me if you need to talk."

"I will," Ginny replied, once she was in the car.

"Oh, wait," Barbara said. "I mentioned Joe's keys to Jimmy a couple of days ago. He said he had them, but he doesn't remember where they are now. Someone used them to drive Joe's truck back to the house last year. And Jimmy doesn't know where they ended up afterward. He was surprised you didn't have them all this time."

Ginny tried to act as unconcerned as possible about that piece of information. "Thanks. I was just...putting away some of Joe's things, and I noticed that the keys were missing. But I'm sure they'll turn up."

"I'd be happy to help you with Joe's things, you know," Barbara offered.

"I know. Maybe one day next week?"

"Sure."

And with that, Ginny escaped. It was pitch-dark by the time she and Hannah made it home. Hannah was wired from the party. She babbled excitedly the whole way. Ginny talked right back, sure Hannah was taking it all in.

"So, you were the belle of the ball, Miss Hannah," she said, slinging the diaper bag over one shoulder, Hannah over the other. "Just ate up all that attention, didn't you, baby girl?"

Obviously pleased with herself, Hannah laughed.

"Now, I know you're all excited about the party," she said, laying the groundwork for what was to come, "but look up into the sky. You know what time it is. You know we both need our beauty sleep."

Hannah gurgled on, feigning obliviousness, now that it suited her.

"And let's not do the 2:00 a.m. thing this morning, all right? That's getting old. Four I can handle, but not two. And we really need to talk about this sleeping-through-the-night thing, Hannah. I swear, all the big girls do that. And you want to be Mama's big girl, don't you?"

Ginny fit her new key in the new lock in the kitchen door, juggled the keys and the diaper bag and the knob. Finally the door swung open. She dropped the diaper bag on the table, turned to lock the door behind her, and then...then she saw it.

Her house...it was trashed. Drawers were hanging open, the contents spilling onto the floor. The cabinets were open, their contents pushed this way and that. Glancing into the living room, she saw more of the same, and felt an awful sense of violation.

Someone had been in her house, gone through her things, taken...Who knew what they'd taken, if they'd even had the chance to leave with anything yet?

Hannah yelped. Ginny nearly jumped out of her skin as she whirled around, checking her back. Finding nothing but the locked door, Ginny turned to Hannah, who had to be complaining because she was being held much too tight. Ginny loosened her hold on the baby and tried to calm herself. She had to figure out what to do next.

Her gaze landed on the phone on the wall by the door. She grabbed the receiver, put her back to the wall so that no one could sneak up on her, then was ready to dial.

Who would she call? The police emergency number came to mind automatically, but she rejected that idea as quickly as it came. Mama Reed listened to the scanner all the time, and if she heard an emergency call go out to Ginny's house, it would frighten her half to death. She'd have a crowd of Reeds here in an instant, and Ginny didn't want to be surrounded by relatives right now.

She wanted...Marc.

Ginny took a breath, tried to take another one, then looked around the room one more time. Marc—that felt right. She wanted him, here, now. And he was only a few blocks away.

Pulling the number out of her head, she dialed. Hannah grabbed for the phone, then fussed when Ginny scolded her too harshly for that.

"I'm sorry, baby," she said as the phone started to ring and her gaze swept around the room from left to right, disbelief still her dominant emotion. "So sorry."

It took forever for him to pick up the phone. She didn't realize how much she just needed to hear his voice until he finally answered.

"It's Ginny," she said breathlessly. "I'm . . . I'm at the house, and . . . someone's been here."

"What?"

"I just got home, and someone's searched the place."

"Did you call 911?"

"No, I called you." She didn't begin to think about what she'd told him right there, or what she'd told herself. She just knew she was frightened, and she wanted Marc. She trusted him to know what to do next.

"Where's Hannah?" He started firing questions at her.

"With me."

"And where are you?"

"At the house, in the kitchen. We came in the back way and found this mess."

"Are you sure the intruder is gone?"

She gasped, scared to even look around the room again, and that must have told Marc all he needed to know.

"Ginny, get the hell out of there, now. Go get in your car. Lock the doors. Pull into the street in front of the house and leave the engine running. If anyone but me tries to get near you, floor it and head for the precinct house on Seventh. Got that?"

"Yes."

"Do it now. I'll be there in four minutes."

Ginny didn't let herself think. She still had her keys in her hand. She left the phone dangling, fumbled the new lock on the back door, which she'd just engaged, then finally got it open.

She and Hannah fled into the night, with Ginny feeling all the while as if the neighborhood had grown eyes, a million of them, that were following their every move. She slid into the driver's seat with Hannah still in her arms. There was no way she was going to give that baby up to the car seat in the middle of the back seat.

Hannah was fussing in earnest now. Surely she knew something was wrong.

"Shhh..." Ginny said, jamming the keys into the ignition, catching her breath when the engine refused to turn over at first. When it caught, she backed into the empty street and pulled against the curb in front of the house.

And then there was nothing to do but sit there and watch and worry. It turned out to be the longest four minutes of her life.

Marc grabbed his shoulder holster, his gun, his shoes and his police radio and took off at a dead run. He chose not to drive because running would just be faster than starting the car and maneuvering through the traffic lights between their homes. He radioed the dispatcher to patch him through to the nearest patrol car as he ran. He didn't think he'd been this afraid since he walked into the middle of that huddle of cops and found Joe lying on the street with blood pumping out of his chest.

He'd made a promise that day to look after Ginny, and he wondered now if there had been more to Joe's request than met the eye.

Had Joe truly done something to put Ginny in danger? Had he feared for her safety as he lay there dying?

Joe had told Marc that he had so many things to say, and he'd seemed to know, too, that he wouldn't have time to say them all. His first concern had been for Ginny.

Take care of her.

Tell her... I'm sorry.

And then he was gone.

Had Joe been saying he was sorry because he'd gotten caught up in something dangerous, something that eventually got him killed? Had he been worried someone would come after Ginny, as well? Was that why he'd wanted Marc to watch over her?

Marc still had trouble believing that whole scenario. But things were starting to happen that pointed in that direction.

Someone had been trying to upset Ginny with that phone call about the bullet Joe fired. Was someone trying to frighten her now by breaking into her house? Please, God, he prayed, let this just be about frightening her.

As he sprinted down the alley, he studied the shadows. A dog barked to his right. A cat hissed, as well. Car horns honked impatiently. Kids' voices carried on the breeze in the early-summer night. There was nothing unusual about the sounds. He saw nothing unusual as he approached the house from the alley. No lights. No windows broken. No movement. With his gun drawn, he rounded the right side and ran down the driveway toward the car.

Ginny saw him and got out of the car. Hannah was in her arms. He looked them over from head to toe as he ran and found nothing awry with either of them. Then he stopped two feet in front of them and had to work very hard at not touching them.

When he saw Ginny sway on her feet, he was actually grateful. He didn't have to hold in check any longer his undeniable urge to touch her. His hands shot out to steady her on her feet.

"Are you all right?" He felt the trembling in her arms.

Ginny nodded and tried to catch her breath. "I was so scared."

"I know." He'd seen too many people shaken up by the idea of someone violating the privacy of their own homes and thinking of what might have happened if they'd been there at the time.

"I just couldn't think," Ginny continued. "And then I didn't know what to do."

Marc felt the urge to give her a lecture on safety right then—namely to never stay inside a building that had been broken into, because you could never be sure the thief was gone. But he didn't think she was up to that right now. Besides, he needed to hang on to her for a few more minutes. "We'll talk about this later, Ginny."

She nodded and kept right on talking. "I probably should have called 911, but your house is so close, and I..."

"I'm glad you called me," he told her. More than glad.

"Good, because now...." She shook her head back and forth. "I feel so foolish, and so...shaken. It seems so silly now. Nothing happened. Still..."

"Yes?"

"Do you think...you could just hold me for a minute?"

Hannah gurgled then, seeming to show her approval of that idea.

"Ladies," Marc said, relaxing a little for the first time since the phone rang and he heard Ginny's breathless voice, "you don't have to ask me twice."

He opened his arms to them and pulled the two of them against his chest. Hannah turned to him and gave him a big smile, then pawed at his face with one stubby hand. Marc kissed the baby on the cheek, but didn't let himself kiss Ginny.

He settled for having her close, knowing she was safe, at least for now. And he had hope tonight, because when she needed help, she'd reached out for him.

So there they were. Ginny was trembling still. Hannah was squirming and babbling about something. Marc still had his gun in his right hand, and they were on a public street with a patrol car on its way, and possibly an intruder inside.

This was not the time or the place to stand here with Ginny in his arms, but he was having a hard time letting go.

"You scared me half to death." He settled for saying that instead.

Ginny pulled back enough that she could look him in the eyes. "Nearly scared myself that much, as well. And Hannah." She kissed the baby's forehead, then began disentangling herself from his arms.

But that didn't happen soon enough.

As Marc turned, a patrol car slid into the driveway, the lights sweeping across the three of them. He could just imagine how their embrace had looked to the two men in the car.

"Come on." He put his arm around Ginny's shoulder and led her toward the car. "Let's see what we have to work with here."

The patrolmen turned out to be two men both Marc and Ginny knew, both the men having worked with Joe at one time or another. Marc gave them a terse description of the situation.

Martinez, the younger officer, asked a few too many questions about exactly who had called the police and how Marc had come to arrive here so quickly. Marc didn't care to answer any of those questions right then and told

Martinez that they all had work to do. They might still have an intruder in the house.

"Reilley," he addressed the other officer, a soft-spoken, freckle-faced redhead, "I want Mrs. Reed and the baby in the patrol car, and I want you to stay out here with them. If we run into any trouble at all, I want you to get them out of here and radio for backup. Got that?"

The man nodded his agreement and turned to Ginny.

"Martinez, come with me," Marc instructed, and walked towards the house, pushing his mind onto the job, when what he really wanted to do was stay with Ginny until she calmed down.

They were safe now, he reminded himself. And he had to figure out what the hell was going on, if he was going to see that they stayed that way.

He and Martinez skirted around the house, finding a broken window at ground level on the left side. "It leads to the basement," Marc said. "The steps come out in the kitchen, behind a door that's normally locked."

Motioning for Martinez to follow, Marc made his way to the back door and the kitchen. They went in with guns drawn, took a quick look around the kitchen, then started searching the rest of the house.

The place was trashed, and it looked as if someone had done a sloppy job, dumping things out of a drawer here, leaving one untouched there. Had the thief been incredibly sloppy? Had he been interrupted by Ginny's arrival? Was this the work of an amateur? Or a scam to keep the police from figuring out what the intruder was actually after?

What could someone want so much that he'd risked trashing the place to find it? Why not search, carefully and methodically, until he found what he was looking for? Why advertise his presence in the house like this?

It didn't make sense. Nothing about this whole mess did.

Still, it did occur to Marc that this was an opportunity that O'Connor and his pals at internal affairs would relish. They could have Joe's house searched from top to bottom, under the guise of searching for clues about the break-in, if they could get their men in without the word going out at the precinct house and without Ginny picking up on exactly who the men were.

Marc didn't like taking advantage of the situation like this. After all, Ginny had been scared half to death. But the case had taken on new urgency for him now. As he saw it, Ginny and Hannah were in danger, and keeping them safe would be his first priority. If searching the house might give IAD some clue it needed to figure out what was going on, Marc wouldn't hesitate to have the house searched.

Someday soon, he would have to make his peace with Ginny on this issue. He was losing all hope that it could be settled quietly, without her knowing anything about it.

Marc turned to Martinez and started issuing orders, the first being to notify the officer outside with Ginny that the house was empty. As Martinez turned to carry out that order, Marc pulled out a handkerchief, wrapped it around the phone receiver and called O'Connor.

Martinez and his partner patched the broken window with a board they found in the shed, and then Marc sent them on their way. He told them he wanted the place searched by a team of officers in the morning, and that it could wait until then. They didn't question him.

Now all he had to do was get Ginny and the baby settled for the night and then return in the morning with a

crew from the precinct to search the place again, so that
no one would get suspicious.

If he could stash Ginny somewhere overnight and keep
the Reeds away for a few hours, O'Connor and his buddies from internal affairs could conduct their own search,
with no one being the wiser.

As the other officers pulled away, he walked Ginny
back inside. Ginny gingerly stepped over the silverware
and pot holders and baby bottles scattered across the
kitchen floor and looked around in horror.

"I can't believe anyone would do this to my house."

"I know." He put a hand to her back to guide her into
the other room, which wasn't as bad as this one. Hannah
was in his arms now, with her head down on his shoulder, where she was purring sleepily.

"Why would someone do this?" Ginny asked.

"Well..." Marc didn't want to tell her, but he couldn't
hide it from her either. "They didn't take your TV, the
VCR, the CD player or the family silver. Do you keep any
jewelry here? Any other valuables? Any cash?"

She looked around, then shook her head.

"I'd say that rules out robbery, although we can't be
sure. You may have scared off the intruder when you
pulled in."

"Oh, God, I don't know what I would have done
if—"

Marc wanted to hold her again, but he didn't think this
was the time. He needed to get Ginny out of the house.
Not just so that the internal affairs team could search the
place, but also for her own sake. She didn't need to be
here right now.

"Come on upstairs. Let's pack an overnight bag for you
and for Hannah and get you out of here."

"Out?" Clearly she hadn't thought that far ahead.

"There's no way I'm letting you stay here tonight."

"Oh."

"Want to go to Mama Reed's?"

Ginny shook her head.

"Barbara and Jimmy's?"

"The whole family's there. At least, they were an hour ago. Barbara had a cookout tonight. That's where Hannah and I were before we came home and found this."

"You're welcome to stay at my house, but ... the family's not going to like it if they find out about it."

"I ..." She seemed ready to accept, then reconsidered. "I don't know, Marc."

"About last night? Or the night before?"

"Both."

"I told you, it doesn't have to change anything between us. I'll still be your friend. I promised Joe I'd look after you, and I intend to keep that promise."

"I still don't know."

"If Joe was alive, he'd never let me hear the end of it if I left you and Hannah alone tonight in this house."

"But ... are you sure?"

"It's late. Hannah's tired, and I have plenty of room." Put that way, it sounded perfectly reasonable, although he knew Mama Reed and the rest of the clan wouldn't accept that explanation as readily.

"If I went to Joe's mother's, she'd fuss over us like you wouldn't believe. She's not going to handle this break-in well."

"Then let's go." He turned for the stairs. Ginny stayed where she was.

"There'll be hell to pay come morning," she argued.

"Ginny, I'll take you anywhere you want to go."

"A hotel?"

"If you like, but I'm not leaving you and Hannah there alone."

"Oh."

"We don't know who broke in here, or why," he said. "But it sure doesn't look like a botched burglary attempt."

"I was afraid of that."

Marc shifted Hannah in his arms. She curled against him and burrowed down into the hollow between his neck and his shoulder, and she felt as if she belonged there. Somewhere along the way, Marc had fallen as hard for the baby as he had for her mother. He wasn't going to let them go.

"You and Hannah will be safe with me," he said.

That seemed to convince her. Ginny followed him upstairs and packed her bag.

Chapter 10

Once at Marc's house, they pushed his bed against the wall, piled pillows on the left side and put Hannah between the pillows and the wall. The baby was asleep before they ever laid her down. Ginny climbed into bed beside her, and Marc prepared for a long night on the sofa.

O'Connor and his crew were probably searching the house right now. Marc wondered if the man would finish the job before someone from the Reed family found out about the break-in and came around to look through the house.

He did call the desk sergeant at the precinct house—thankfully, someone he knew and trusted to be discreet. Marc instructed the man that if any of the Reeds called, asking about Ginny or the break-in, he should direct their calls to Marc. He didn't give the desk sergeant any further information.

Marc figured it wouldn't take long for someone to show up on his doorstep, and then he and Ginny would have a lot of explaining to do. This time, it wouldn't be so easy. He could no longer say with a clear conscience that nothing had happened between them.

He'd kissed her, twice now, and he wanted to do much more than that. One of Joe's brothers would probably hit him. Mama Reed would cry and make Ginny feel guilty. No one would understand. And the family would close in around Ginny to protect her from him. They'd forget that he had loved Joe like a brother. He'd be nothing but a man trying to move in on Joe's wife.

Marc poured himself a fresh cup of coffee and sat in the darkness of his living room. He must have fallen asleep, because the next thing he knew, hours had passed and Ginny was standing in front of him.

He closed his eyes. The image was too outlandish to be real. Ginny Reed in his house, in his bed, in the middle of the night. How would he ever sleep in that bed again without dreaming of her the instant he drifted off to sleep? It would be torture—sweet, sexy torture.

When Marc opened his eyes, he tried not to stare. She had on the pink robe, the collar of a white cotton pajama top visible underneath. Bottoms, too. He had to check. Once he was this far gone, what did it matter? Her hair was tousled, the curls a sexy mess that begged to have his fingers stroking through them. She looked so shy, so innocent, so uncertain. He felt like a heel for ever telling or showing her how he felt.

"Sorry," she said. "I didn't mean to wake you."

He shrugged. "No problem."

Ginny hesitated, looked more uncertain than ever, then said, "I know it's late, but do you think we could talk?"

If they could keep it to talk. "Sure." He moved over to the other end of the sofa.

She sat on the opposite end, turned sideways and tucked her legs up under her. "You know, when you came to the house the night before, we kind of got sidetracked."

Marc laughed. "Delicately put, Mrs. Reed."

She looked taken aback. And he realized it was because he'd never called her anything but Ginny, not ever.

"I'm sorry," he said. "You want to talk about Joe and bullets that weren't where they should have been and husbands who weren't acting the way they normally did?"

"Yes."

"We can talk about that. And that reminds me, did you ever find out where Joe's set of keys went?"

"No, I didn't. Jimmy remembers getting them and the envelope with Joe's things in it, and giving the keys to someone so they could pick up the truck. But he doesn't remember which of the guys it was. And nobody remembers seeing the keys since then."

"So did you have the locks changed?"

"Yes. Yesterday morning. But what does that have to do with anything? You said someone broke into the house through the window in the basement."

Someone had broken the window, and someone had busted the lock on the door leading from the basement into the kitchen. That didn't mean he hadn't had a key that suddenly didn't fit the locks. Or that someone hadn't already used that key in the past. Maybe he hadn't found what he was looking for the first time. Or maybe he'd gotten worried now that Ginny was asking questions. Maybe he'd broken in to take another look around in case he'd missed something the first time.

Marc looked at Ginny and tried to evade the questions in her eyes as best he could. "I'm just thinking out loud," he said, wondering how many more lies he'd tell her before this was over. "Who did you ask about the keys?"

"Mama Reed, Ben and Barbara."

"Anyone else?"

"No, but I told you, the whole family was together tonight, and you know how Mama Reed likes to talk."

"And did you ask about the other things? Did you tell anyone we were after the notebook?"

"No. They wouldn't understand that I was asking questions about Joe."

"Or that I'm helping you."

"I don't want to cause trouble for you," she said.

"And I don't want to cause trouble for you, but I have, just by bringing you here tonight."

Ginny tucked a stray curl behind her right ear. "It's going to be ugly in the morning. They just don't understand. Mama Reed thinks I should be living with her and Joe's father indefinitely. And this break-in is going to change everything."

"It does change everything," he said. "And I'm not talking about Mama Reed. Think about it, Ginny. Someone called you and told you about the bullet from Joe's gun. You and I start going through his things, looking for those missing keys, and the next thing you know, someone breaks into your house."

"You think there's a connection."

"I stopped believing in coincidences a long time ago."

"Still, you said I might have interrupted the burglar when I walked into the house."

Marc shook his head. "I know you'd like to believe that, but someone had to have been in your house a long while in order to search through that many of your things. Most burglars are in and out in a matter of minutes."

"Oh."

"Ginny, I don't want to scare you, but I want you to know what you're up against. I don't think it was someone looking for the family silver. And I want you to be cautious. I know bringing you here is going to strain your relationship with the Reeds, but that's not my top priority right now. Keeping you safe is. And I will do whatever I have to do to keep you safe."

Ginny drew her knees up to her chest and slid her arms around her shins. "I feel safe here with you. That's why I came."

"Good." It was better than good, actually. He found it incredibly satisfying that she'd turned to him.

"Now it's my turn to ask the questions," she said. "What do you think the break-in means?"

"It could mean a lot of things."

She looked as if she were going to question him further on that subject, so he continued, "Ginny, if I knew anything for sure about this break-in, I'd tell you. And anything less than that would be sheer speculation."

"Let's speculate."

"Let's not."

"I'm still hearing things about those crooked cops."

Marc tried out his best poker face on her. She wasn't buying it.

"People are wondering if Joe was one of them."

"Why would they shoot him if he was one of them?" Marc could have answered her a dozen different ways, but he thought this was his strongest comeback. It was what he kept in the forefront of his mind whenever he had doubts about Joe.

"They had some sort of argument? They wanted him out of the way? He made them nervous?"

"Then they'd never shoot him on a public street in the middle of the day with a couple of FBI agents looking on.

Come on, Ginny. Joe was a cop. When cops get killed, it tends to attract a lot of attention.''

''You didn't say you think Joe had nothing to do with those men.''

''I didn't think I had to say it. I don't believe Joe would do anything like that. You don't believe it, either.''

''No, but some people might.''

''I hope it doesn't come to that,'' Marc said.

''To where people are speculating about what kind of a man and what kind of a cop he was?''

''Yeah.''

''But you know things you're not telling me.''

He nodded, then paused, trying to hold himself back. It didn't work. Marc slid across the sofa, put his right arm along the back of the cushion behind Ginny and took her chin in his left hand, forcing her to look him in the eye.

''I want you to understand this. I need for you to understand it. I believed in Joe. There were things happening at the end that I can't explain, but I still don't think he could do anything illegal. I hope you believe that, Ginny.''

''I do. And I believe in him, too. I'm worried, and I have questions, but I don't believe the things some people are saying about him.''

Marc nodded. ''Now, as I see it, I have an obligation to him, to see that nothing tarnishes his memory and to see that you and Hannah don't get hurt. Those are my priorities. That's the reason I brought you back here tonight.''

''You really think we're in danger?''

''I'm not sure what's going on, but I'm going to proceed as if you and Hannah are in danger.''

''Oh, Marc. How did it all get so complicated? How did it ever come to this?''

"Someone's trying to get to you. They're either trying to intimidate you or just to start trouble. Someone broke into your house tonight, either looking for something of Joe's or just because they're trying to shake you up. I don't know why, or who's doing it, but I'll find out. And I bet the answers to those questions will tell us a lot about what was going on with Joe those last few months."

She didn't say anything, but she looked more troubled with each passing moment.

"Ginny, you have to promise me you'll be careful."

"I will," she said. "And...I don't know what to say or how to explain to you what it means to me to have you looking out for Hannah and me now."

"You don't have to say a thing."

"I do. It means a lot to me."

"And you mean a whole lot to me." He looked away before he could read her reaction to that announcement in her eyes. But he still held one of her hands in his, and she was only inches away.

"I've always felt close to you...." she began.

He flinched, and thought it was definitely time to try to lighten the mood. "Is this going to be one of those 'You're a great guy, but I just want to be friends' speeches?"

"I'm not sure."

"Because it's not necessary. I know my timing's lousy. I know what's going on in your life right now. I didn't tell you how I feel to make you uncomfortable, or to put you under any more pressure than you're already feeling."

Ginny licked her lips. Marc took it like a blow to the stomach. He sucked in a breath and looked away.

"Then why did you tell me?" she asked.

"I didn't see the point in trying to hide it any longer, and after kissing you the other night, I thought I'd made my feelings rather obvious anyway."

"Oh."

"You don't think I make a habit of kissing women like that in their kitchens?"

She shrugged helplessly, and color crept into her cheeks. She looked very kissable right then.

"Ginny," he said, unable to help himself as he took her chin in his hand and leaned toward her, so that he could look directly into her eyes, "I have my standards, you know. Just ask anybody. I'm not easy."

That did the trick. Laughter bubbled up inside her and overflowed. She smiled, as he hadn't seen her smile in a long time. And the sight of her nearly took his breath away.

"I'm relieved, of course."

"Besides," he said, defending himself, "that kiss was incredible. At least it was for me."

Ginny just sat there. One moment he thought she was going to make a run for the bedroom. And the next...the next he saw definite possibilities in this whole situation.

Marc swore.

"What?" she asked, so innocently.

"I made myself a promise the other night."

"And that was?"

"I promised I wasn't going to push."

"Oh."

"I promised myself I wasn't going to touch you, and I'm about to break that promise."

She licked her lips once again. It started a fire deep in his belly, one that he was sure would become a roaring blaze the minute he touched his lips to hers.

"You're not making this any easier," he groaned, when she didn't move. "And I swear, you're the most beautiful woman I've ever seen."

She just stared at him then. Her hair was a mess, a beautiful, soft, curly mess. Her eyes were big enough for him to drown in. He wanted her so much it was becoming embarrassing. He was surprised she hadn't noticed by now. The situation was definitely getting out of control, and it was up to him to do something about it.

He'd brought her here with nothing but the most honorable of intentions, and here he was, dangerously close to kissing her. It hadn't taken more than a few hours before he sank to this level.

Marc summoned up every ounce of self-control he possessed. "Ginny, go back to bed."

"What?"

So innocent. So bewitching. She was killing him, bit by bit. "I mean that if you're still sitting here beside me thirty seconds from now, I'm going to kiss you again."

Ginny didn't move. She couldn't. It was as if he'd cast a spell over her and left her paralyzed with nothing more than the sound of his voice and the look in his eyes. That odd mix of excitement and desire, so intense they couldn't possibly be real, served to keep her exactly where she was.

It's the newness, she told herself. The difference. He was the first man, besides her husband, that she'd kissed in more than ten years. Of course she would find that exciting on some level.

Still, she seemed to find it exciting on just about every level she could imagine.

And she was relieved that he'd been so forthcoming about himself. Quite honestly, she hadn't been sure whether he made a habit of kissing women like that or not. Oh, she'd thought she knew. She'd never heard anyone talk about Marc running around with lots of women, the way so many men did. But she'd needed to hear him say that the kiss had been special to him, that she was special, too.

"I think I'm totally out of my depth here," she confessed, wanting this particular admission out of the way. "You've probably figured it out by now, but...I just wanted you to know. Joe was...he was the only one. Billy Reynolds kissed me on the cheek one time at some party my freshman year in high school, and I bloodied his nose trying to get away from him. But that was it."

"You bloodied Billy Reynolds's nose?" Marc moved a fraction of an inch closer when he said it, and he was already too close for comfort.

"Yes." She could feel the heat coming off him. She knew the strength of his arms, the feeling that she was safe there. Yet, at the same time, when he got this close to her lately, she could be hanging over a precipice a mile wide and just as deep, with him her only lifeline.

It was heady stuff, intoxicating, enticing, and it all served to pull her ever closer to him.

Marc smiled. Now what had she said that would make him smile? Ginny shook her head, the movement sending an errant curl across the side of her face. He brushed it away, his hand lingering near her hairline, then slipping in amid her curls.

"Anyway," she said, breathless now, "he was the only one. Except for Joe."

"And me."

Her lashes fluttered down. Her heart faltered once, then again, until she felt dizzy. His lips, as warm and smooth and inviting as she remembered, settled over hers. She couldn't hold back a sigh that held some mixture of surprise and resignation.

It felt every bit as good as before, maybe even better. Her hands, balled into fists in front of her, came open and found the muscles in his arms. She knew the width of them, and their strength, so well now. And then she let her hands settle lightly against his shirt. His heart was pounding; thank goodness hers wasn't the only one. Sliding her hands higher, she found his shoulders and clung to him.

As his lips roamed freely over hers, he turned her in his arms, until she faced him, then settled her more firmly against him.

Ginny felt the tips of her breasts pucker up and jut against his chest; he had to feel that, too. She tried to pull away, but he protested.

"No," he said, against her lips. "Not yet."

Then he took her mouth, thrusting deeper. His arms were so tight around her, they were nearly crushing her. Or maybe she just couldn't breathe anymore. That could be it. That could be the reason her head was spinning, that he was the only solid thing in her world. That could be the reason she wished she would never have to let him go.

Everything about this whole mess was so complicated, so uncertain, so frightening. But here, with him, life was deceptively simple.

Marc Dalton was crazy about her, and she didn't think she ever wanted to leave the shelter of his arms. She didn't want to think about tomorrow, or the day after, or anything else except this moment with him.

Ginny gave herself over to the kiss. One of her hands was in his hair, the other against a slightly rough-feeling jawline, and she was in heaven. She was.

She heard ... The phone was ringing.

Marc swore, then eased her back until her head was resting against the back of the sofa. His gaze blazing down into hers, he brushed her hair back, then let his fingertips linger against her cheek. His breath was as ragged as hers.

Ginny glanced at the clock on the wall. It was 4:20. Hannah would be awake soon, and wanting a snack. And the phone wouldn't stop ringing.

"You know who that is," she said.

He winked at her and tried to summon a smile. "Give me three guesses," he said.

"I'll get it."

He waved her off. "No way I'm going to let you deal with them right now. Just give me a second to catch my breath. And you stay right where you are."

His hand was still against her cheek. She turned in to the warmth of his caress and sighed. How far would they have gone if the Reeds hadn't found her? What would she have let him do? And how would she have felt about it in the morning?

Marc reached out and silenced the phone. "Close your eyes, so this won't be an out-and-out lie," he told her, then said into the phone, "Dalton."

"What the hell is going on there?"

Ginny could make out Jimmy's voice. He was yelling.

"I'm just sitting here waiting for you to find me."

"And Ginny? Do you have her with you, too?"

"And Hannah," he said.

Jimmy calmed down a little from there. Either that or he gave up shouting. Ginny couldn't hear any more.

Marc said, "Hang on a minute." Then he brushed his hand over her eyes until her lashes fluttered down. "She looks like she's sleeping," he said into the phone.

Ginny had to fight to hold back her laughter, and she realized that she'd laughed more in the past few days with this man than she had in years. When had she forgotten how to laugh? When had she forgotten how good it felt?

And how could she be laughing now, when she was going to catch hell from the Reeds in the morning?

Marc was trying to reason with Jimmy. "Look, it's not that hard to understand. She didn't want to have to deal with twenty different people tonight. She was tired. Hannah was nearly asleep already. There was no way I was going to leave her alone until we figure out who broke into the house. So I brought her here and put her and Hannah to bed."

Jimmy must not have been in the mood to listen to reason, because Marc kept talking. "It's not that hard to understand, Jimmy."

And from there the conversation went downhill quickly. Marc hung up the phone a minute later.

"Guess it is that hard to understand," Ginny said.

"Yeah."

"Is he coming over here now?"

"I don't know. I tried to convince him to wait until morning, to let the two of you get some sleep, but he wasn't exactly in an accommodating mood."

"I'm sorry, Marc. I shouldn't have put you in a position to have to defend yourself, or me."

"You know what?" He let his hand slide down the side of her face, then traced a finger across her lips. "I'd do just about anything for you."

Her heart started thudding again, and she didn't want to move from this spot. She wanted to hide away with him here and lock the rest of the world out, just for a few moments. It was so tempting it frightened her. And things were moving much too quickly.

"Marc," she began, trying to back off, "I don't know what—"

His fingers, pressed against her lips, silenced her. "You don't have to say anything to that. I just wanted you to know."

"Thank you."

He let his lips claim hers again for one dizzying instant, then helped her right herself. He nodded toward the bedroom. "You're supposed to be asleep, remember? I'll try to keep him away from you until morning."

"Thanks," she said, heading for the bedroom, to wait for her daughter to wake up and demand to be fed.

Chapter 11

Jimmy didn't waste any time. Fifteen minutes later, he was pounding on the door.

Marc pulled the door open and wondered if the guy would throw a punch at him. He didn't—not at first, anyway. But he definitely seemed to be considering it.

"Hannah's asleep. So's Ginny. Do you think we could do this without raising our voices?" Marc was in no mood.

"What the hell is going on here? And what's with you? Joey was your friend."

"And you think he wouldn't be anymore because his wife and his daughter slept in the other room, rather than at their own house, after someone broke in and scared them half to death?"

"Yeah, and you stay at his house because Hannah's too sick for Ginny to manage on her own?"

"What do you want? A copy of the doctor bill? Or maybe a look at the prescription bottle? The baby was sick, and Ginny was exhausted. I happened to be there. I happen to be a friend. What should I have done?"

"Called the family."

"The family, namely your mother, is making Ginny a little crazy right now, and I think you, of all people, should understand that."

Jimmy flinched. It was no secret that Mama Reed's interest in Jimmy and Barbara's marriage had caused quite a bit of friction in the first few years. "She means well," Jimmy said.

"I didn't say Mama Reed *meant* to make Ginny crazy. I said she *was* making Ginny crazy."

"Look, she's just concerned. We all are."

"And the clan, collectively concerned, is enough to smother somebody. Damn, Jimmy, why can't you be reasonable about this? Give Ginny a break. Ask them to back off."

"So you can move in on her? Joe's barely even been dead a year yet."

"I know exactly when Joe died. I was the one who was with him when it happened." Marc had to fight against letting that image settle in before his closed eyes. And when he could see straight again, he added, "I'm not sleeping with Joe's wife, okay?"

"You looked awfully cozy that morning in her kitchen."

"Well, I've only had coffee in that kitchen a thousand times or so. I guess I've gotten a little comfortable there over the years. Remember when Joe and I pulled the graveyard shift for two years straight? Guess where we ended up for breakfast? Joe and Ginny's."

"Hey, it just doesn't look good, okay?"

Marc could have backed off right then. He could have apologized and kept his distance for a while. He couldn't bring himself to do that. He'd declared his intentions to Ginny. He might as well start paving the way to do that with the rest of the Reed family.

He was here to stay, if she'd have him. The family might as well get used to it.

"You know what was on your brother's mind the last few moments he was alive?"

"Why don't you tell me about my brother?"

"He was worried about Ginny."

"Oh, yeah?"

"He asked me to look after her, and I'm going to do that. Nothing, not you or your whole family, is going to stop me from keeping that promise to Joe."

"Ginny has a family," Jimmy argued.

"Joe asked," Marc repeated. "And I gave him my word." He hoped that would settle it, but it didn't.

"And while you're watching over his wife, you're going to make a move on her, as well?"

Marc tried not to let any emotion show. Not the guilt. Not the anger. Not the frustration. He had a job to do here. He was going to do it.

"I'm worried about her, and if you'd stop being so damned unreasonable about this, you would be, too. Think about it, man. Someone broke into her house, but they didn't steal anything. They left two thousand dollars' worth of stuff in plain sight."

"So she interrupted them as they were getting started."

Marc shook his head. "They had time to search the place."

"Then what was it?"

"I don't know, but I plan to find out."

"Your guys go over the place yet?"

"Just quickly. We'll cover it this morning."

"How's Ginny?"

"Scared. And confused. You could make it easier on her. Talk to your mother. Get her to back off. And get Ginny to stay with you and Barbara so she doesn't have to go back to the house right away."

Jimmy looked a little sheepish. "I guess I could do that, for Ginny."

"Good. Thanks."

Jimmy nodded grudgingly. Marc wondered how much power Jimmy or anyone else had over Mama Reed. And he wondered if there was a chance in hell of the family accepting any relationship between him and Ginny, or if they'd always see that as a betrayal of her marriage to Joe.

Jimmy, true to his word, managed to hold off the horde of worried and angry Reeds. At eight-thirty, Barbara phoned to say she'd be happy to come by and pick up Ginny and Hannah, if they wanted to spend the night.

Marc had Hannah in his arms. She was hunkered down against him, trying her best to get a mouthful of his shirt to chew on. Marc was humming to her while he stood in the kitchen stirring some hot oatmeal, which Ginny said Hannah liked now.

Ginny came in, dressed in her jeans and a pink shirt with a wide lace collar, her hair still damp from the shower. She hesitated for a moment in the kitchen doorway, then came to take Hannah from him.

"Thanks for hanging on to her while I got dressed." Hannah lit up at the sight of her mom. She gave her a big smile, then tugged on a handful of Ginny's hair.

"No problem," Marc said, beating Ginny to the job of untangling her hair from Hannah's grasp. Ginny went still beside him. She looked up at him and caught her breath as he settled his lips against hers in a quick, soft kiss. "Good morning."

"Morning," she said breathlessly, not backing away, but not inviting him to come any closer, either.

One step forward, one step back, Marc thought, determined not to let that discourage him. He poured Ginny some coffee.

"Barbara called," he told her. "She said you're welcome to stay with her and Jimmy for a few days."

"Do you think that's necessary?"

"Well, we'll go over the house today to see if we can lift any prints the intruder might have left. And we'll need you to check more closely to see if anything's missing. I'll call someone about getting the window repaired, and it wouldn't be a bad idea to get some bars put on the basement windows. It's too easy to bust one and slide in when they're that close to the ground. That could take a couple of days."

"And you think I shouldn't go back until that's done?"

He nodded. "Besides, if you go back today, you'll be overrun with Reeds. I think you'd find more peace and quiet at Barbara and Jimmy's."

"Okay. To tell you the truth, I'm a little frightened by the idea of going back there today, anyway. Do you think I should get an alarm system?"

"A dog with a nasty bark could do the trick."

"Oh, I hadn't thought about that. I bet Hannah would like that much better, wouldn't you, little girl?"

Hannah started babbling, going on and on, as if she were making perfect sense to both of them. Ginny laughed and kissed her daughter's forehead.

"I guess that's settled," Ginny said. "We'll find a dog."

"I know someone who breeds Labs. I'll get his number for you."

"Thanks. I appreciate that. I appreciate everything you've done for us. I don't know how to thank you."

"Just be careful," he said. "And don't ever hesitate to call me if you need help, even if you just don't want to walk into that house at night alone for some reason."

"I can't be afraid to walk into my own house."

"But you will be, for a while. It's only natural, after what happened last night."

"Still, I—"

"No, you promise me, right now, at the first sign of trouble, the first instinct that tells you something isn't right, you'll call me. Or at least call someone. Otherwise, I'm going to camp out in my car in the street in front of your house. I'll make the Reeds look like distant relatives, for all the room I give you."

"What?"

"You heard me. And don't go getting all indignant on me. I'm not implying that you aren't capable of taking care of yourself."

"I think that's what you just did."

"Ginny, why do you think we have cops? Because lots of people find themselves in situations they can't handle alone. I'm not insulting you, I'm just worried about you."

"Oh."

"Okay, I may be a little overprotective where you and Hannah are concerned." He waited, letting that settle in, then added, "You're just going to have to get used to that."

"I think I might have something to say about it."

"You want to argue that point? Fine. When we catch the person who broke into your house and the one who called to tell you about the bullet from Joe's gun that nearly hit the FBI agent, then you and I can argue about this urge I have to protect you. Until then, it's settled."

Ginny cocked her head to the right and stared at him, amused or angered, he couldn't say for sure which.

"How is it that I've totally missed this arrogant, autocratic side of you before now?"

"I've been hiding all sorts of things from you," he said, grinning at her, and then kissed her again before she could summon a protest. Pulling away long before he was satisfied, he said, "I'm hoping you'll get used to that, too, because I intend to make a habit of it."

"Oh, you do?"

"Any objections to that?"

He waited, wondering if he'd overstepped his bounds and honestly offended her.

"I'm going to have to think about this," she said, "when you're not kissing me."

"Fair enough. Just promise me you'll be careful."

"I will."

"First sign of trouble—"

"I'll call." She hesitated, then added, "You."

Ginny had a hectic day with Hannah. Later she got the baby settled at Barbara's, confessed to Barbara that Marc had kissed her, but revealed nothing else at first. But surely the look on her face when she made that particular confession said it all. Luckily, Barbara took pity on her and gave the subject a rest.

Around noon, Antonio came to Barbara's and picked her up, then took her to the house, where she gathered a few more clothes and some of Hannah's toys. Antonio told her the crew had found no evidence that would help them find the intruder. And he asked her to look through the place to see if anything had been taken.

Ginny was in the bedroom she and Joe shared when she came upon the little red notebook. It was lying in the midst of a pile of items emptied from the boxes of Joe's belongings that she and Marc had dumped in the walk-in closet. Excited, she glanced at the notebook's date—three months before Joe's death—then slipped it into her purse, hoping Antonio didn't notice. Marc would be happy to see this.

"Find anything?"

Startled, Ginny whirled around and tried to lie. "No. Nothing seems to be missing. At least not from what I can tell. Maybe after I put the place back together, I'll see that some things are missing."

"Maybe," Antonio said.

"I appreciate you bringing me over here like this. I'm still a little shaken up."

"No problem," he said.

Ginny took a good look at Joe's cousin and shook her head. Antonio wore an earring—a small gold ball—that Mama Reed had hit the ceiling over. Off duty, he wore his pants a little too tight, his shirt open a button or two too far, and a gold chain around his neck. He drove too fast, drank a little too much, stayed out too late. Mama Reed found his behavior downright scandalous, and she gave his mother—her sister, who had married one of Joseph Reed, Sr.'s, cousins—fits about it.

Still, Antonio had settled down lately, since joining the force.

"How many months have you been a patrolman now?" Ginny asked, trying to make conversation and take her mind off the shape of her poor house.

"Coming up on eighteen months." He smiled at her, as she was sure he smiled at all the women, as if expecting her to swoon.

Ginny laughed. She couldn't help it. Antonio always had thought a lot of himself.

"What is it?" he said.

"Nothing. Really. I'm ready to go, if you are."

He turned and leaned against the door with his shoulders. "You know, I've been hearing things about you and Dalton."

"Oh?" Ginny didn't believe she was going to get the third-degree from someone who was at least five years younger than she was.

"Uh-huh." Antonio nodded. "I've been hearing things about him, too, around the precinct house."

"And what have you heard about Marc?"

"Maybe nothing. Maybe something. Too soon to tell. But Joe gave me a piece of advice when I got my badge. He said to keep my ears open, to listen carefully to anything anyone had to say, and that it's a mistake to dismiss anything out of turn without checking it out."

"Joe said that?" Antonio was going to try to damn Marc in her eyes with words from her own husband?

"Sure did."

"So what are you telling me?"

"Just be careful," Antonio said cryptically. "He may not be the man you think he is."

"And what's that supposed to mean?"

"It means I hear things, and I don't have a blind spot where the man's concerned."

"And I do?"

Antonio shrugged, as if this all meant nothing to him. "I don't want to see you get hurt."

"Marc would never hurt me." She had no doubts about that. "Or anyone."

"Maybe. Maybe not."

"Exactly what are you trying to say? You heard something that may or may not mean anything, from someone whose name you're not going to give me. And based on this, I'm supposed to—what? Steer clear of a man I've known for practically my entire life?"

Antonio shifted his weight from one side to the other and still managed to look perfectly relaxed. "Hey, I'm just saying that I'm not sure you can trust him. You can do whatever you want. I just thought I owed it to you to pass this on. That's all."

"That's ridiculous." Ginny would trust Marc before she trusted Antonio, any day of the week, but she didn't see the need to share that with him.

Antonio, cool, confident, unconcerned, shrugged his shoulders. "Just something to think about."

"Okay, I'll keep that in mind." Ginny held her temper. Just barely. "Now, if we're done, I think I'd like to get back to Hannah."

Antonio drove her to Barbara and Jimmy's. Hannah was just getting ready for her afternoon nap. Ginny fed her, changed her and put her down in the spare bedroom in the portable crib that Barbara had. Then she walked into the kitchen where Barbara was making sandwiches.

"I hope you're hungry," her sister-in-law said, "because I have strict orders from Mama Reed to see that you're fed. Or else."

Ginny took the plate Barbara offered and put it on the counter, beside the stool. "Or else what? She'll come over and force-feed me?"

"I wouldn't want to risk it, if I were you. Eat."

"I'm just going to get a glass of milk. Want one?"

"Sure." Barbara took her own plate to the counter and sat down. "How did it go at the house?"

"The place is a wreck. Every bit as bad as I remembered last night. Maybe worse."

"And nothing was missing?"

"No."

"Ginny, I don't like the sound of that."

"Neither did Marc."

"What do you think's going on?" Barbara took the milk Ginny offered, then started to eat.

Ginny stood there, her stomach in knots, and wondered if she could get a bite down that would stay. "I don't know what's going on." Not wanting to talk about it further, she decided to try to change the subject. "But I had the strangest conversation with Antonio at the house."

"Oh?"

"He warned me away from Marc."

"What?"

"Isn't that the craziest thing? He said he's been hearing things around the precinct house, and he isn't sure if I should trust Marc."

"That is crazy," Barbara said.

"I know."

"He's probably just doing his bit to get you away from Marc."

"That's what I thought. But do you think someone would put him up to lying about Marc that way to try to change my mind about him?"

Barbara perked up. "Oh, you've made up your mind about Marc?"

Ginny smiled, the mood broken. "Yes. I trust him, Barb."

"Oh."

"Oh, hell, you're as bad as the rest of them."

"No, I'm not. I'm your friend, and I'm curious. That's all. Tell me more about this kiss."

Ginny tried with all her self-control not to blush. It didn't work. "He kissed me. What is there to say?"

"Oh, I don't know. That the earth moved or something?"

"Well . . . it was nice."

"Nice? A gorgeous man like Marc kisses you, and it's nice? I don't think so, Gin."

"All right. It was more than nice. It was really nice. And once I got over the shock, I liked it."

Barbara looked thoroughly disappointed with that description of the events.

"Okay, I liked it a lot."

"And the earth moved," Barbara prodded.

Ginny wavered. It was probably a lost cause, judging by the heat flooding her cheeks. She might as well admit it. "Okay, he's incredible. He kissed me, and I felt like a schoolgirl again. I could have melted into a puddle at his feet, it felt so good. If I hadn't been holding on to him, I probably would have fallen down."

Barbara had the nerve to look smug, as if she'd known the answer all along.

"Are you satisfied now?"

"No," Barbara replied. "Are you?"

As a matter of fact, Ginny wasn't satisfied at all. That afternoon as she sat in the spare bedroom nursing Hannah, she was having all sorts of daydreams, involving more than a kiss from Marc. And somewhere inside, she was ashamed of herself for that. But the shame was quickly giving way to all sorts of rationalizations.

Joe was gone. He wasn't ever coming back. Would she be betraying him and their marriage by becoming involved with another man? Was the guilt coming from the fact that Marc had been Joe's friend and partner? Or was it so strong because it had only been a year since Joe died?

Would she feel any less guilty a year from now, if she and Marc started seeing each other? Would the family accept it any more easily then than they would now?

Ginny sensed that it would never be easy. Whoever she dated, whenever it happened, the family would not like it.

But she kept thinking of what Marc had said the night of Hannah's baptism, about finding a father for Hannah. Watching her daughter now, Ginny knew she did want Hannah to have everything. A photograph and the name of a man who would never hold her in his arms, never be there to share a single day of her life, would not be enough.

Ginny had had a photograph and some memories. It hadn't been enough for her.

Still, remarrying? The idea had sounded absurd when Marc first mentioned it, but now that she'd thought it through, it seemed like the most reasonable thing in the world. Ginny would do anything for Hannah.

And there was only one way to find a father for her daughter. She would have to find a husband for herself.

But she wasn't talking about some marriage of convenience here. She was talking about herself, and this sudden, growing desire she had for Marc.

If there was going to be another man in her life, she could only see one man in that role.

Marc.

Of course, he hadn't mentioned anything like marriage. He hadn't done anything more than kiss her and confess that he was crazy about her. What in the world did that mean?

She could just see herself asking Barbara about that. Come to think of it, Barbara had been married even longer than Ginny had. She wouldn't be any help at all in interpreting for Ginny. She'd have to figure out Marc's intentions all on her own.

And she needed to see him, anyway. She still had Joe's notebook tucked away in her pocket. Marc would be anxious to see it.

She had the perfect excuse to go see him. And Jimmy was working some sort of late duty tonight. He wouldn't have to know she was at Marc's. Barbara would cover for her.

Ginny was tempted, sorely tempted.

When Marc turned Ginny and Hannah over to Barbara Reed that morning, he'd barely had a chance to say goodbye—at least not the kind of goodbye he would have liked. Barbara was watching them the whole time. He'd wondered how long it would be before he saw her alone again. He'd wondered how much it was possible to miss a woman who hadn't been gone for five minutes yet.

As the day wore on, he found out. Marc took the least experienced evidence crew he could find to search Ginny's house. If any of the Reeds had gone by the house that morning and seen the earlier search by the internal affairs crew, they hadn't mentioned it to him yet. Maybe IAD had gotten away without being noticed.

As expected, the crew he searched with found nothing. He'd intended to be at the house that afternoon when Ginny walked through to make sure nothing was missing, but he'd been called away instead.

By the end of the day, Marc was no closer to figuring out who had broken into Ginny's house or why. Because she was at Jimmy and Barbara's house, he couldn't just stop by and see her. It would cause even more talk.

He tried to concentrate on his job, on the mystery that Joe had become in death, and on his calendar, which showed the trial looming ever closer.

None of that worked. He just kept thinking about Ginny. He thought about kissing her. Actually, he thought about more than that. As the clock crept forward, he saw no reason to even think about going to bed—he wasn't going to be able to sleep.

Shortly after nine, the doorbell rang. A grim-faced O'Connor stood on the back step. Mark knew instantly, from the expression on O'Connor's face and the fact that the man had come to his house, that something was terribly wrong.

"Come inside," he said, closing the door behind O'Connor and checking to see if anyone was watching.

O'Connor didn't take the seat Marc offered. He stood by the door.

His stomach in knots, Marc asked finally, "How bad could it be?"

"Bad. During our search at Joey's house we found a knife in the basement. It had a ten-inch blade, serrated edges, and was stained. We took it back to the lab. I didn't even mention it, because I didn't think we had a hope in hell of coming up with anything from it. And because... well, you know I think the people who believe Joey was dirty are crazy."

O'Connor looked as if he were having trouble finding the right words. Marc remembered that the man standing in front of him had gone through the academy with Joe Reed, Sr.—he had close ties to the Reed family.

"Anyway," O'Connor continued, "we checked out the knife. The stain was blood."

Marc swore. "So, he had a knife. He cut himself on it one day and didn't clean it."

O'Connor shook his head. "Joey was B positive. The blood on the knife was AB negative—pretty rare stuff. Guess who else was AB negative."

"No way," Marc said.

Renata Leone, the woman whose throat had been slit before she was left to die in an alley on the North Side last year had been AB negative?

"Yeah. Hell of a coincidence, huh?"

"Come on," Marc argued. "Joey was a cop. No cop would slit a woman's throat, then throw the bloody knife in his basement."

"Doesn't seem like it."

"Oh, hell. You know he wouldn't. And the woman's son already IDed Morris as her killer, anyway."

"He said he saw Morris standing over his dead mother's body."

"And then Morris just happened to try to kill the boy and anybody who happened to be near the kid. I think that's a pretty good indication that Morris was the man who murdered Renata Leone."

"But he hasn't been convicted of that. Technically, the case is still open."

"Only because the DA has a stronger case against Morris for murdering Joe, and because his chief witness in the woman's case happens to be a little boy who's, what, eight? Nine?"

"Nine," O'Connor said.

Marc shook his head. "We know Joe didn't kill that woman."

"Yeah, but you and I know Joey wasn't a crooked cop. Other people aren't as certain about that, and I don't have to tell you what they're going to do with this bloody knife."

Again Marc felt his stomach twist and turn inside him. He knew what some people could easily do with this piece of evidence. The investigation against Joe Reed was about to go public in a big, big way. After all, IAD had found the knife. It wouldn't take long for that piece of information to get out around the station, and that was all it would take. Everyone would know Joe was being investigated, and Joe's enemies would get their wish.

"They'll crucify him," Marc said.

Chapter 12

Marc was afraid of what he would find in the headlines
tomorrow morning. More importantly, he was afraid of
what Ginny would find.

He couldn't let her find out like that. He wanted to be
the one to tell her. It would come as a blow to Joe's entire
family, and he didn't want her to be in the middle of dozens of hurt, angry, outraged relatives when she found out
about the investigation.

Still, he wondered if anything could make this easier to
hear, wondered if it would matter to her at all that he was
the one who told her? O'Connor was going to call the
family together tonight and break the news. Marc had no
time to waste.

Marc pulled up to Jimmy and Barbara's house, then
walked to the back door and knocked. Ginny and Barbara were in the kitchen, putting away the supper dishes.

"Hello, stranger," Barbara said, teasing him.

Marc tried to summon a smile. He turned to Ginny. "Is Hannah down for the night?"

She nodded. "What's wrong?"

He shrugged and tried not to look so glum as the two women stared at him. "Barbara, you can handle this by yourself for a while, can't you?"

"Sure."

He took Ginny by the hand and motioned for her to follow him.

"Marc?" she protested, as he led her out the door.

Ginny stopped before she'd taken three steps onto the sidewalk, and he could see that she wasn't going to budge until he told her something.

"Aw, Ginny," he said, his heart aching at the thought of what she was about to learn. And then, because she still looked so beautiful and so incredibly appealing to him, he took her by the arms and pulled her close for the space of maybe two seconds and kissed her.

She didn't fight him, and that was something he took as a good sign in an otherwise bleak evening. But the way she looked at him—so trusting—cut right down to his soul.

"What is it?"

"Not now," he begged. "I'll tell you ev—"

He caught himself before he made a promise he wouldn't be able to keep. He wasn't going to tell her everything. O'Connor didn't think Marc's job was done, and besides, the stakes were higher than ever now.

"I'll tell you what's happened as soon as we get back to my place, okay?"

Ginny nodded, and together they drove off into the night.

Marc remained silent on the drive, but he managed to take Ginny's hand in his and hold on tight. This was his worst nightmare coming true—she was going to find out about the investigation of Joe.

But now that Marc was faced with that moment, he knew he feared something else even more. Selfishly he feared the day she found out about his involvement in this whole mess.

Ginny was coming to trust him, to rely on him. Maybe even to love him a little. Or was that all wishful thinking on his part? Because, sitting beside her in the car, the darkness closing in on them, her hand clasped warmly in his, he knew that he loved her.

Probably he always had. He'd kept hoping it was some sort of adolescent crush and that someday, he'd meet a woman a lot like Ginny, a woman who could be his, as he thought Ginny never would.

Damn, he thought, it had been almost a dozen years since he'd fallen for her. A dozen years he'd been fighting his feelings.

Sooner than he would have liked, they were in his driveway. Without a word, they made their way inside. Marc took the phone in the kitchen off the hook. He turned on a single lamp, the one in the corner of the living room, then offered Ginny a seat on the sofa, while he stood by the fireplace and searched for a way to begin.

"Did you find the other woman?" Ginny finally said.

He whirled around to face her. "No, of course not. Ginny, there is no other woman."

She looked away, and he caught the glint of tears in her eyes. Marc swore and took a seat on the coffee table in front of her, a move that put him at eye level with her. "The man was in love with you. Absolutely, positively, in love, Ginny."

She shrugged and looked away. "I just...I couldn't figure out what else you would find so difficult to tell me."

He took her hands in his, needing the contact. "I'm sorry. I thought we'd put that whole idea behind us."

"I'm trying to," she said, looking as miserable as Marc felt.

He didn't say anything for the longest time after that. He couldn't. Finally Ginny pulled her hands from his. "Well, before you spring your news on me, I need to tell you mine." She reached into the back pocket of her jeans and pulled out a little red spiral notebook, which she handed over to him.

Marc forgot about what he had to tell her in his excitement at the sight of that little book. "If this is what I think it is..." This could be it—just what he needed, especially now that the knife had been found.

He opened the notebook to the first page, saw Joe's nearly illegible scrawl and a cryptic mix of initials and numbers, then whistled. "You don't know how much we need this right now." Hoping the answer might be significant, he asked, "Where did you find it?"

"At the house this afternoon," she said, excited now. "The intruder must have uncovered it when he trashed the place."

Not likely, Marc thought. IAD had been warned to be on the lookout for a small red notebook. They wouldn't have missed it.

"Exactly where was this?" he said, wondering if she'd just handed him something as damning as the bloody knife.

"In the closet where Joe's things are."

Marc had searched that area himself with the second evidence crew. The notebook hadn't been there. He felt a nasty shiver work its way down his spine.

"Ginny, this is important. You found this lying in plain sight, this afternoon, when you went through the house?"

"Yes." She seemed wary now. "It was on the floor, in a pile of stuff that came out of one of the boxes where Joe's stuff was stored. Why? I thought you'd be pleased."

That depended on what was inside the notebook.

"Marc, what is it?"

He took her hands in his. He had no more time for stalling. Even now, O'Connor would be arriving at Jimmy and Barbara's, having called the family together to tell them. Marc wouldn't be surprised if someone came looking for Ginny after that. They wouldn't take kindly to the fact that she was with him and he'd been the one to break the news to her.

"Marc?" she asked, more urgently than before.

"I'm sorry. This is difficult for me."

"For me, too. You're really scaring me now."

"I'm getting scared myself." He let go of one of her hands to pick up the notebook again. "This wasn't at the house early this morning. I went through it with the evidence crew myself. I searched Joe's closet because I didn't want anyone else to know that all of his things were in there. The notebook wasn't there."

She hesitated, not liking what she was thinking. "I don't understand. If it wasn't there then..."

"Someone put it there after the evidence crew left. Someone wanted you to find it. Or someone knew we were looking for it, knew we'd be suspicious if we couldn't find it. So they returned it."

Ginny paled. "Why?"

He shrugged. "Maybe they thought we'd stop digging if we found the notebook, particularly if there was nothing unusual inside it. Maybe they made sure there was nothing to find in the notebook, so there was no reason not to return it."

"But . . . what does that mean?"

"It means someone is awfully nervous at the idea that we're looking into Joe's death. And I'm afraid it doesn't have anything to do with this idea of yours that Joe was involved with another woman."

"Oh." Ginny swallowed hard, put a hand to her throat, then over her mouth. He thought she was going to cry.

Marc took her right hand in his and found that she was trembling. "You've heard the rumors," he said. "About Joe?"

Ginny was having trouble breathing. She had a childish urge to hide and hope that this whole thing was some sort of nightmare that would end as soon as she woke up. One look at Marc's tense features told her this wasn't the kind of nightmare that came to an end with the rising of the sun.

"I don't believe they're true," Marc said.

She realized she'd needed to hear him say that. "But this is more than just talk now, isn't it?"

"I'm afraid so."

Ginny dreaded the next part. With all her heart, she dreaded it. "What happened tonight? What is it that you're so afraid to tell me?"

When he didn't answer her right away, she asked, "How bad can it be?"

"Bad." He was through mincing words.

"Okay, tell me."

"You remember Renata Leone?"

"The woman found dead in the alley? The same woman who was killed by the man who murdered Joe?"

"That woman. I know Morris killed her. I have no doubts in my mind about that. The woman's own son will testify to that, if he has to."

Ginny nodded, though she didn't see the connection. "So? What does Joe have to do with that woman?"

"When your house was searched today, after the break-in, we found the knife that we think was used to kill Renata Leone."

Ginny was certain she hadn't heard him correctly. She tried to get her hand loose from his, but he refused to let her break the connection between them. And then she decided she was glad for that, and she held on to Marc as tightly as she could. His touch, his strength, steadied her, while the room turned at some crazy angle around her, in a way that left her feeling dizzy and light-headed.

"The knife used to kill that woman was found in my house?" she managed to ask.

"Yes."

Ginny shook her head. "But that doesn't make any sense."

"I know."

"How can you be sure? How do you know that's the knife that killed her?"

"There was still some blood residue on the blade. We typed it. Renata Leone had a very rare type, and it matched."

"No," Ginny said, ready to beg him to tell her this wasn't true.

"And...it's not your ordinary household knife. It had a huge blade, serrated edges. It... Dammit, Ginny. I'm so sorry about this. The blade matched the wounds on the woman's neck."

For a minute, Ginny thought she was going to be sick. By sheer force of will alone, she fought back her nausea and forced herself to think. Joe had always said there was an answer to everything, if you could simply think things through.

"It... Still, it doesn't make sense. Why Joe? You said you know who killed that woman. It's the same man who killed Joe. So why would the knife be in our house? And why would it matter, anyway, if it was?"

And then she remembered the bullet, the one that had landed in the wrong place, the one fired from Joe's gun that day on the street. She remembered that Morris was a desperate man, that he was a cop, and that he thought to ruin Joe's reputation in a desperate attempt to save himself.

"Are you...are you saying...that someone thinks my husband was involved in that woman's death? That this has gone from a ridiculous innuendo about my husband being a crooked cop to the point where he's being linked to a murder?"

"I'm sorry," Marc said. "I never wanted you to have to know."

Still Ginny was incredulous. "How could anyone honestly believe Joe could do such a thing?"

"I don't know what they have."

"They?" Her mind locked on that word. "Who is *they?*"

"Internal affairs," he answered. "They've opened an investigation—on Joe."

Ginny felt herself slipping sideways, falling, then found herself caught firmly in Marc's arms. He held her tightly for a few moments, then reluctantly let her go and went to the kitchen. He came back quickly, a bottle and glass in his hands.

Marc poured her a glass of brandy, and she swallowed it, feeling the liquid burn all the way down. When she had pulled herself together enough to think, she was deadly calm. She would not let herself think of what he'd told her, not yet. Instead, she chose to focus on what she would do next.

"Does the family know?"

"Someone's telling them now."

One question down. "What about the TV people? And the newspapers?"

"I don't think anyone's going to call a press conference about this, but you know how these things go. Someone will leak the story, and when they do, you're going to want to be out of sight for a few days."

Ginny nodded. She vaguely remembered the TV lights, the cameras and the microphones from Joe's funeral, and she had no desire to go through something like that again.

"It might be a good idea to go to the house tonight and pack some things," Marc suggested. "You didn't take that much to Barbara's, did you?"

"Just clothes for two or three days."

"I'll go pack for you, if you like, but I'm not crazy about leaving you alone right now."

"I don't—" Ginny had to stop and breathe. She didn't want to be alone. She didn't want to be without Marc. It was something that was becoming easier and easier for her to accept.

"Ginny?"

She looked at him. Really looked at him. What in the world would she be doing right now, without him? She felt better simply being in the same room with him.

And she wanted....what? What more did she want? "I don't want to be alone right now. I'll come to the house with you."

* * *

The house was deserted, and everything was still a mess from the break-in. Somehow, it didn't feel like her house anymore. And she kept thinking of that bloody knife in the basement.

Marc found a couple of suitcases. She put him to work in Hannah's room, directing him to the essentials the baby would need. Ginny grabbed her own clothes, not caring what she wore, and threw them into another suitcase. When she was done, she moved into the bathroom and threw some more essentials into the case. Then she made the mistake of wandering into what she'd come to think of as Joe's room.

Photographs of the two of them were still on the walls here. His clothes, his favorite baseball glove, his running shoes, were in the first heap of things piled on the floor.

Ginny tried to imagine strangers—or maybe they hadn't been strangers, because she knew so many policemen— combing through her house, searching for something that would prove her husband had been a dirty cop.

She remembered little of the madness surrounding the arrest of two policemen and an FBI agent last year following Joe's death, but over the years, she'd seen such things happen. It didn't happen often, just frequently enough to make people who depended on the police force for their own safety distrust all policemen for a while.

It made life difficult for every cop in the city for a long time, and there was nothing a dedicated policeman hated more than a dirty cop.

Would they think of Joe that way now? Could the people who'd known him, who'd worked with him and his family for years, ever believe that about Joe?

It would have hurt him terribly to think that they could. It would hurt the family, as well.

When Ginny started this whole mess by asking Marc for help, she'd never imagined anything like this coming out of those final, confused days with her husband.

Oh, she'd caught a glance from someone from time to time, one that told her some people might be saying ugly things, but she'd accepted that. Some people were always eager to believe there was bad in everyone. Ginny had dismissed those looks as nothing but cynicism.

So she'd never let herself believe for one minute it might be true. She'd never searched her own heart to see if that might actually be the reason for Joe's odd behavior.

She turned when she heard footsteps coming up behind her.

"Ready to go?" Marc asked.

She nodded, not trusting herself to speak right then. "My suitcase is in the bathroom."

"I've already taken them to the car."

"Oh." She must have been absolutely lost up here with her troubling thoughts.

"I got through to Barbara. She's going to slip out of the house with Hannah and bring her to us."

"Good." She liked the thought of having Hannah in her arms right now.

"Let's go," Marc said.

She didn't talk to Barbara, because she didn't think she could manage to do so without breaking down. And she couldn't hear about how the news had affected the whole family. Maybe tomorrow, but not tonight.

Barbara thought to pack Hannah's portable crib, and Marc set it up in the spare bedroom he used as an office. Hannah woke up just long enough to eat her fill, then drifted off again. Ginny held the baby for about twenty minutes more before putting her down. Then she went in search of Marc.

Now that Hannah was down for the night, Ginny remembered that she and Marc hadn't even discussed the idea of them staying here with him. He'd just assumed. Or maybe she'd assumed. What had he said after he told her about the internal affairs investigation? That she'd want to disappear for a few days? She wondered if that included getting away from him, as well.

She didn't want to do that. Marc had become a lifeline to her. And even though she knew she shouldn't let him walk in and take charge of her life like this, she thought she just might let him. For a few days, she told herself, or maybe a week. She'd be stronger then.

Ginny walked into the bedroom she and Hannah had shared the last time they were here and found Marc with her suitcase.

"Would you—?" she began, then stopped, her throat so tight it hurt, her eyes flooding with tears, then overflowing.

He seemed to understand just what she needed, what she wanted. He held out his arms and caught her up in them. When her knees gave way, he picked her up and carried her the three steps to the bed, then settled her in his arms again, her head on his shoulder, and let her cry it out.

Everything she'd been holding in for weeks, maybe even for the past year, seemed to have exploded within her, then settled on her chest like a weight that might well crush her.

She pictured Joe's face the last time she'd talked to him, that morning when he'd left for work, when he'd told her he might need some time to get his head on straight.

Where in the world had his head been that morning? What kind of secrets had he taken to his grave? What secrets were opened up for the whole city to see?

"Joe's not... He wouldn't have done such a terrible thing," she managed to say.

Marc's hand captured her chin, then gently tilted her face up to his. "I don't believe it, either. We'll fight this thing and prove he didn't do anything wrong."

Suddenly the temptation to lean on him was too great to resist any longer. Ginny burrowed in closer to Marc and let her tears fall. "It's so... it's so unreal, so unfair...."

"I know." Marc held her tight. His hand stroked its way down her hair in a gesture so comforting she wished she could stay in his arms forever.

All her energy seemed to have disappeared; all the courage she would need to fight off this new threat was gone. Marc was the only solid thing in her world.

And then he kissed her. He pulled back just enough that she caught the sight of his lips coming down toward hers, had just enough time to close her eyes, before his lips landed on her cheek and he started kissing away her tears, his touch as soft and gentle as the baby's. Ginny felt just as much love in the feel of his lips on her face as she did when Hannah gave her those silly, sloppy play kisses that babies gave, and something inside Ginny began to shift and turn.

They hadn't talked about love; she hadn't even considered loving again or having someone's love to call her own. Surely the whole concept should frighten her. Surely it should remind her of all she'd loved and lost.

But she had no fear now.

Love—the idea, the emotion—pulled at her like a beacon as seductive as the feel of this man's lips against her own or the iron band of his arms wrapped protectively around her in the dark.

Right after Joe died, the last thing she'd wanted was someone else to love. It had seemed too much of a risk to take. Then Hannah had come along, and drawn it out of Ginny as naturally and as easily as the baby smiled and cooed and crooned to her. There was simply no denying it. She loved Hannah. She always would.

And now the thought of a man's love, the temptation of it, the seductive draw of it, hit her.

Marc brushed the pads of his thumbs past her eyelashes, down the sides of her face and into her hair, which was wet with tears. So softly, so tenderly, he smoothed back her hair, letting his hands rest there. He watched her, first focusing on her eyes, then on her mouth.

Love wasn't the only thing tempting her now. Even as that idea formed, Marc's lips started a slow journey across her now closed eyes, down the side of her face and into her hair, following the same path his fingers had taken only moments before.

Ginny's breath caught in her throat. She was suddenly conscious of the fact that the two of them were in his bedroom, stretched out on his bed, and that she was in his arms. His touch soothed at first, comforted, and then it took on a whole new dimension.

Something crackled in the air, an awareness of lines being crossed that they hadn't even approached before, of their relationship shifting irrevocably into uncharted waters. They were headed for waters even more treacherous than those they'd broached with his kisses and his puzzling yet altogether seductive admission that he was crazy about her, that he had been for years.

Marc's lips blazed a path from the side of her face to her neck, his touch still light, his intent now clearly to

arouse rather than to comfort. Ginny meant to protest.
But her hands and her body seemed to have a mind all
their own. Her fingertips slid into his dark hair, amid the
curls, where they dared to urge him closer still, and her
body arched treacherously into his until she almost cried
out from the pleasure.

Surely there were a million things that should be racing
through her head right know—like the fact that she
shouldn't be doing this, that she had no idea what his intentions were beyond where they were clearly headed tonight in this bed.

It felt so good to be close to another person, to forget,
for a moment, everything but the feel of his arms and his
lips, now heading for her mouth.

She opened to him, made one desperate grab for air,
and then felt his mouth take hers. There was an urgency
to him now that at any other time would have frightened
her. But in this moment she felt the urgency in herself, as
well.

She wanted this man. She wanted to give this night over
to him, to follow where he led, to find out what would
become of this thing between them, from which she could
no longer hide.

Ginny knew he would never hurt her, never betray her.
She would be safe with him, and yet . . . on another level,
maybe she wouldn't.

Maybe he would turn out to be as dangerous to her
heart as Hannah.

Hannah had demanded that Ginny come back to life,
and Ginny had. Now Marc wanted a whole different part
of her resurrected, as well. And she didn't know if she had
the will to deny him that.

The way he touched her, the way the muscles bunched
in the sensual columns of his arms, the way his rock-hard

thighs slid between hers, the way his mouth had of generating lightning heat wherever it touched her—this was different.

"Marc?" she said, breathless, when he finally pulled away. His body was lying on top of hers. His arousal, big and hard and throbbing against her belly, left no doubt in her mind where this was leading.

He pulled his mouth from hers, then let his forehead come down to rest lightly against hers as he sighed heavily. "Ginny, it's all right. I've waited forever for this. I can wait a little longer if I have to."

"I don't want to let you go right now," she said.

"Then don't," he said wickedly, conjuring up all sorts of images in her mind.

He kissed her once, giving her added incentive. She kissed him back, because she wanted to so much, and because it managed to buy her a little more time.

There was no doubt in her mind that he would give her all the time she needed, and yet she had other needs, as well. She needed him, and not just to hold her in his arms. She wanted to feel like a woman again, wanted to know that the totally feminine part of her hadn't shriveled up and died in the past year. She wanted to know that she could once again have everything she had had in her first marriage, by starting over with someone else. Maybe she could even have more than that this time.

And, plain and simple, she wanted Marc. She kissed him again, letting herself just feel. His lips were warm and soft, and the taste of him was as sinful as the finest of wines. It was late, and he hadn't shaved. His jawline was hard, the skin raspy. The heat coming off him was enough to set her on fire if she wasn't careful.

Trouble was, she'd been careful and cautious her whole life. She didn't want to be careful tonight.

"I do want you, " she said, a little shocked to hear the words come out of her own mouth.

Marc smiled against her lips. His chest expanded in a move she could only call proud. Still, he told her, "I can wait. I mean it. Just say the word, and we're done. At least for tonight."

"You'll ... you're not ..." How in the world did a woman ask this question?

Was he serious about her? Of course he was serious about making love to her. But would they be making love, or would it be something else, that didn't mean nearly as much? Would it just be need and desire and the natural inclinations of a man who found himself in bed with a woman?

"What is it, love?" he whispered, his lips against her ear enough to set her to shivering all over.

Love? Did he? Did she dare hope?

"Love?" she said, as softly as she possibly could.

Chapter 13

Marc rolled off her. She heard his feet hit the floor, saw his back to her for a minute, then blinked, surprised, as he snapped on the bedside lamp and light flooded the room.

Obviously, she thought, they weren't going to have this conversation in the dark.

Ginny's face burned, and she had trouble meeting his eyes. She felt more than saw him turn sideways and lean into the bed above her, his shoulders blocking out the worst of the light. Swallowing hard, Ginny imagined those shoulders, that bare, broad chest, his weight balanced on those arms in which she felt so safe, his body surging into hers.

It had been so long...so very long. Her mouth went dry, and she turned away from him, because she was afraid he could read the thoughts running through her head.

Marc wouldn't have that. He came closer, until she put her hands against his chest. He made quick work of the buttons of his shirt, then guided one of her hands inside, until her palm was flat against his skin, his heart thundering beneath her hand.

"I just have one question," he said.

"Okay."

"Is there any doubt in your mind about how much I love you?"

She was speechless.

"Ginny?" He smiled when he said it, and a beautiful light came into his eyes, as if he had gotten great satisfaction from simply saying the words. "A man doesn't wait forever for a woman if all he wants is to have sex with her."

"He doesn't?" she managed.

Marc shook his head, his gaze never wavering from hers.

Like a quick flash of heat, love—the idea of it, the wonder and the awe—settled over her. It lingered in the air between them, its presence almost a tangible thing.

"I didn't think I had to say it," he murmured.

"Please, say it."

He put his lips to hers. "I love you, Ginny."

His kiss then was as slow and as sensuous as anything she'd ever felt in her life. It was a smooth, soft exploration of her mouth, a stroking of her tongue that became an erotic promise of things to come. And he set her whole body to throbbing, started this ache between her thighs—with just that kiss.

"Don't ever doubt what I feel for you." He said it like a pledge, like a sacred oath.

Ginny didn't doubt that, not now. He wouldn't say he loved her unless he was absolutely sure about that. The problem now was her own feelings for him. "Marc, I can't... I mean, I'm not..."

"You don't love me?"

She flinched, not wanting to hurt him, but not wanting to mislead him, either. "I'm not saying that. I'm just so confused right now...."

He didn't seem nearly as troubled by that as she was at the moment. "Hey, don't worry. I can wait for that, too, if I have to."

"Oh."

He smiled at her obvious relief. "Ginny, you're forgetting, I've already waited so long. What's a few more weeks? A few more months? You take as long as you need. I'll be right here waiting when you make up your mind."

She nodded slowly, wondering how she'd managed to have two exceptional men fall in love with her. "I care about you," she felt compelled to add. "A great deal."

He winced, pulling away, his hands making a theatrical play of covering his wounded heart. "Not that. Anything but that."

"No, I mean it. And not like *that*. I ... Marc, everything is just so crazy right now."

"I know, sweetheart." He turned all serious on her again, and one of his hands slid down the side of her face.

Ginny closed her eyes, savoring the warmth of that touch, the reassurance and the gentleness that was so clearly his intent.

"It won't always be like this," he promised her. "We'll come through to the other side of this whole mess. Everything will come clear in the end."

"I know it will."

"And I'll promise you one thing. I'm going to make you so happy."

"Oh, Marc." She had tears in her eyes again.

Ginny wrapped her arms around him, pulling him closer. She tilted her head to one side and shivered as she imagined, then felt, his lips exploring further. His teeth sank into the side of her neck, gently, erotically. And then his mouth closed over the pulse point there, the feeling shooting through her and sending her arching up off the bed, gasping out his name.

The sensations, like the colors of the rainbow, exploded in vivid detail, and she didn't want them to end.

Marc was still sitting on the side of the bed, leaning over her, balancing his weight on his arms. Ginny's hands slid once again inside his open shirt, finding a mat of crisp, brown curls and more muscles to uncover. His chest, his shoulders, those arms she loved so much. She pulled down the shirt, then had to undo a handful of other buttons to take it any farther.

He loved her. He wasn't just fooling around here. And she trusted him. If she was ever going to be with another man, it would be Marc. If she was going to spend the rest of her life with someone, it was clear to her in that moment, that man would also be Marc. What else did she need to know tonight?

The thought that there was no reason to wait excited Ginny. It excited her almost as much as Marc's mouth did. She wanted him so much, and she trusted him with her life—with her daughter's life, even. There was nothing more important to her.

Briefly Ginny thought about the changes wrought in her body by that much-loved baby girl of hers. The pounds, the stretch marks, the pieces that just didn't fit together anymore the way they used to. She thought about the light shining from the lamp in the corner, the man who'd confessed to loving her in one breath and in the other told her he could wait for her as long as it took.

Try as she might, Ginny just didn't see the need to wait. Suddenly she knew what she needed to do.

"Marc?"

He took that to mean that she wanted him to stop, and he did. Groaning, he dragged his lips away from hers after settling a series of kisses, each softer and lighter than the previous one, along her neck, across her cheek and finally, to her mouth.

Breathing hard, his lids low over his eyes, something she read to be a combination of satisfaction and regret mingling there, he smiled at her. "Sorry. I'm getting a little carried away here. You do that to me."

"You don't have to be sorry," she said, then considered all the places she wanted to feel his hands on her body.

Ginny held out her hand to his. She watched as their two hands met, his sun-browned hand so much bigger, so much stronger, than hers, yet so gentle. Just as his hand closed around hers, she wanted her body enfolded in his. She wanted that now, tonight.

Closing her eyes, drawing in a deep breath that did nothing to steady her or to slow her thundering heart, she guided that hand to her breast.

The heat hit her even before he touched her. The weight of his hand, the slight roughness of his skin as he took his thumb and teased the center of her breast, surprised her. She'd wanted his touch there, so much, but the reality of it was even sweeter than she'd imagined. Her body seemed to come alive beneath his hand, taking on a life of its own. She couldn't breathe, couldn't move, could only feel.

"Ginny?"

She had her hand over his, holding it in place, arching into his touch, waiting for him to take her other breast in his other hand, imagining nothing between them and no holding back.

"Marc, turn out the light."

Marc froze, unable to fulfill that tantalizing request, working hard to think with a brain that was simply overloaded with sensation and longing.

"Are you sure?" he managed to say.

She nodded. Even if she hadn't spoken a word, he could have read her answer in her body. If it was possible, her heart was beating even faster than before, her breathing becoming even more agitated. Beneath his hand, her breast was soft and swollen, the center jutting up at his touch, begging for more. Her hand was on top of his, holding his there, welcoming him, urging him on when he needed no urging at all.

His first thought was that if he was dreaming, it was the best dream he'd ever had.

Hell, it *was* every dream he'd ever had.

"Ginny?"

He put his lips to the base of her throat, then followed the line of her blouse downward. One button, then another, and he was in the smooth, sweet-smelling hollow between her breasts. Whichever way he turned, he would find one of them, his for the taking.

Still, he lifted his head one more time, because he wanted to look at her, to imprint this memory in his brain forever—Ginny, about to become his.

"I won't let you go," he told her. "Once I make you mine, that's it. It's forever, as far as I'm concerned."

"Marc?"

He was almost afraid to answer her. "Yes?"

"Turn out the light."

The light was gone. His only regret was that he had to take his hands off her for a second to do it. When he looked back, into the shadows, he saw that Ginny had her hands at the neckline of her blouse, undoing one of the dainty little buttons.

He stilled her hand with his own. "That's my job. My pleasure, I should say."

Then he had what he suspected would be his last lucid thought. "Just give me a second."

He pulled open the top drawer of the nightstand, dug through it for a minute, then found what he needed. He threw one of the small plastic pouches on the nightstand, then turned back to her.

Where did he start, when there was so much he wanted to do, so much he'd imagined doing? He thought about it, all the while feeling like a kid on Christmas morning, seeing that he'd been given exactly what he wanted but finding himself afraid to reach out and take it, afraid of finding out it wasn't quite real.

His hand, when he reached for her, was trembling. He didn't care if she felt it, if she knew how deeply she affected him. He fumbled the next button on her blouse and had to try it again, finally managed to free them all. The snap of her bra was in front, and it came loose without a fight. One hand slid underneath the white lace, his hand cupping the tender curve of her breast as her undergarment had a moment before.

Ginny sucked in a long breath when his fingers slid inside, but she didn't protest. For a moment more, he let his conscience needle him. It was too soon for her to be sure about this, and it was probably wrong of him to even consider making love to her tonight, after all she'd been through.

But he wanted her so much. He needed her, and he'd waited for her for so long.

She didn't love him, not yet, but love would come. He didn't think she'd be here in his bed if she wasn't half in love with him already. Marc wanted to use his body and hers to bind the two of them together even more. He wanted her to ache for him the way he'd ached for her. He wanted her to remember how it was between the two of them when the whole family started raising hell about them being together and when Ginny found out what he'd been doing with internal affairs.

Was that wrong of him? To make love to her tonight, with those two reasons high on his list of motivations? Put that way, it sounded manipulative as hell. But he wanted her, any way he could get her. Once he made love to her, he wasn't going to let her go.

While his conscience was warring with itself, she was melting. Her breast swelled into his hand, begging for his touch. Her eyes were closed, and her expression was one of the most beautiful sights he'd ever seen. He could do anything he wanted to her right now, and she would let him.

When he stripped off the last of her clothes, he'd find her wet and ready for him; the thought was nearly his undoing. He was through wrestling with his conscience, at least for tonight. Let it give him hell tomorrow, if that was how it had to be. For tonight, he was going to be with Ginny.

Marc brushed the bra aside and, inch by precious inch, lowered himself to her, until those creamy-soft breasts were nestled in the hair on his chest. He laughed softly, then groaned. There was no way he was going to make this last.

Ginny had her hands on his upper arms, and her nails sank into his biceps as she moved against him, her body undulating, its message unmistakable. She wanted him, too.

If it was possible, he was even harder than before. His arousal strained against the zipper of his jeans, to the point where it was almost painful. Marc took her lips, groaning against them, then plundering with his tongue. Thrusting into her mouth, he imagined how it would be, soon, when he was inside of her.

He rolled sideways, taking her with him as he went, so that while he kissed her he could get a hand between them and touch her, anywhere he wanted. He took her breast in his right hand and tried to ignore the ache in his jeans. He wanted her naked and beneath him, wanted himself naked and buried inside her, but there were so many other things he wanted to do first.

Somewhere in the back of his mind was the nagging fear that this might be his only chance, that if he only got to do this once, he'd damned well better make it last.

He let his lips trail down to one of her breasts, brushing them lightly with his tongue, taking the weight and the measure of them with his hand. Ginny gasped. Her hands were in his hair, pulling him to her. Their legs were intertwined now, that knot of desire growing ever tighter. He put a hand to her hips, palming one, guiding her into a rhythm that would be his undoing. He was nearly gone right now, and they still had their clothes on.

"Careful," he warned her, as she nearly caught fire in his arms.

Marc had to pull away long enough to fumble with the waistband of her jeans, slide down the zipper, then pull them off her. He tried not to even look at that narrow scrap of lace between her legs, the only thing covering her now, tried not to imagine the way it would feel to sink into the very heat of her.

Without looking, he stripped her of her last remaining garment, then went to work on his. His pants were gone. His briefs followed. While he still had the forethought, he ripped open the plastic pouch and pulled on the condom. Soon, he promised himself, he wouldn't need that. Soon, there would be nothing between them.

He lay back down beside her, and she turned in to his arms. The satiny softness of her skin glided along his heated flesh, nearly turning his renewed resolve to take this slow into nothing more than a starving man's wish.

Women like her were meant to be savored, he told himself. And first times—first times were meant to be that way, as well.

Marc stared at her lips, again, this time with their bodies locked together, nothing and no one between them. She was trembling. Before too long, he was, as well. Soon their arms were locked around each other, their legs intertwined, and his desire was at the same fever pitch it had been only moments before.

He trailed one hand down the side of her body, then up the front of her thighs, which parted willingly for him. His hand sank into those curls, and then he entered her with one finger, finding her wet and ready, as he'd known he would.

Ginny mumbled something that sounded like "Please."

"Please what?" he said, trembling with the effort to hold himself in check.

Her hands were locked on his hips, urging him closer. "Now," she whispered. "Please, now."

They were the sweetest words he'd ever heard. He rolled on top of her, positioning himself between her legs, then waited there, on the brink of everything he'd ever wanted.

"I won't let you go," he said. "Not now. Not ever."

"Marc, I don't want you to let me go," she answered, drawing his body down to hers.

It was torture. Sweet, seductive torture. The muscles in his hips tensed as he moved forward an inch, testing to be sure she was ready for him. Ginny's nails sank into his back. She made little whimpering sounds in the back of her throat, and then she was twisting and turning beneath him. Her legs opened wider, taking him in deeper still.

He was right there, right on the brink, his heart hers for the taking right now, his dreams about to come true. He looked down at her; her hair was spread across his pillow, and her eyes were dark and deep enough for a man to drown in. He lifted himself away from her, seeing her breasts, her belly, looking lower still, to the point where his body was entering hers.

"Ginny," he said as he pushed inside her.

Every muscle in his body went tight, stretched to the point of snapping in two, as he fought for control and to hold this position. The heat hit him first, then the exquisite pressure of being inside her. She was tight enough that he wondered if he'd hurt her, wondered if he'd waited long enough. But she was also slick with what could only be desire. She was hot, steamy-hot, and this was torture, the sweetest torture he'd ever known.

He moaned and hung his head until his lips again found the hollow of her throat, then the rim of her ear. "You are so beautiful," he whispered. "Absolutely beautiful. And you feel so good, Ginny. You're killing me, little by little."

She answered him by drawing him closer still. He thrust against her once, the pressure simply exquisite; he didn't know how he could possibly hold out against the sensations bombarding him.

"Please," she said, her hands on his hips, urging him on. "Please."

But he was determined to wait for her. Gritting his teeth, he settled into the rhythm that he hoped would push her over the edge. Rocking against her hips, thrusting deeper and deeper, he took one of her breasts into his mouth. He played with the nipple, tugging, nipping, sucking on it, until an answering pressure built between her legs. She rose up off the mattress as the contractions hit her. He would have sworn she was surprised by it, and a satisfaction like none he'd ever known washed over him.

Ginny trembled beneath him, the muscles deep inside her gripping him in waves now. He thrust once, then again, then gave in to the madness of it himself, with her name on his lips.

Chapter 14

From somewhere far away, Ginny heard Hannah crying, but she merely snuggled deeper into the bed at first. Her face buried in the pillow, she caught the unfamiliar whiff of cologne and sweat—an absolutely masculine scent.

In her bed?

She rolled over in the darkness and blinked twice at the sight—the old brass headboard, the pale taupe walls, the clothes littering the floor, her bra, her shirt, her jeans...someone else's jeans.

Ginny wasn't in her own bed. Looking down at her body, she saw that she didn't have on a stitch of clothes, either.

The night before came back to her in one nearly blinding burst of sensations—Marc's mouth on hers, his hands stripping her of her clothes, his body hot and hard and insistent against hers. She remembered the sound of her name on his lips, remembered her fingernails digging into his back when she'd thought she was drowning and he was the only one who could save her.

Ginny swallowed hard, blinking away the images, thinking instead of the moment at hand. She wasn't embarrassed—not exactly, anyway. Just...hesitant. She had no idea what to expect.

Then Marc walked in the door. A startled glance told her he hadn't bothered to put on anything except his underwear. In his arms was Hannah, looking for all the world as if she belonged there. But once she caught sight of her mother, Hannah remembered her hunger and started howling for all she was worth.

Curiously, Marc was smiling through the whole thing.

Ginny, searching for something to say, started with that. "You like being awakened like this at 4:58?"

His smile only broadened, taking on a devilish aspect. "I like seeing you in my bed. Naked."

She grabbed for the nearest piece of clothing she could find, which happened to be his shirt, and shoved her arms through the sleeves. As the scent of him enveloped her along with the cloth, she wondered if she'd just made a mistake. After all, she needed no reminders of exactly how it had been between the two of them the night before.

Concentrating on her hungry baby, Ginny propped a pillow against the headboard, leaned back against it, pulled the covers over her lap and placed another pillow there. Then she reached for her daughter, who'd turned red in the face and was whimpering by then.

She took Hannah, tensing only a little as Marc's hands brushed against her arms in the process of handing over her daughter. He was watching her every move as she pushed the ends of his shirt aside and bared one breast for the baby, who latched on greedily and began to suck.

In what had become an instinctive motion by now, she kept one arm around the baby and, using her free arm, pressed her wrist against her other breast, to keep the milk where it should be until Hannah was ready to switch sides.

Marc stood by the side of the bed as he watched her nurse the baby with an expression on his face that she would have sworn was pure satisfaction.

"You know," he said, "the first time I watched you do this, I ached for hours."

Ginny turned red, her face flaming, her body aching in places she'd forgotten existed. She felt the bed give as he sat down beside her, felt Marc's lips, soft and warm, against her cheek, near her right ear. "Tell me you don't have any regrets about what's happened between us, because I need to hear that right now, sweetheart."

"Not regrets."

"Guilt?"

"Maybe."

"We shouldn't have to feel guilty about being happy," he said. "Ginny, tell me you're happy."

"I am. I guess... I'm just having a little trouble taking this all in. It happened so fast, I'm still a little dizzy."

"I know. Me too. I meant for us to wait, but..."

"I know you did. I... I don't know what possessed me to..."

"Turn out that light?"

She nodded, her face burning. She didn't think she'd ever been so bold.

"I'm not objecting," he added. "I just wasn't sure what kind of reception I'd get this morning."

Ginny smiled then. "And you got Hannah, the howler, at 5:00 a.m."

He chuckled. One of his hands reached out to stroke the baby's cheek. Startled, Hannah forgot her breakfast for a moment and turned to stare at him. Her mouth and her chin were wet with milk, and her eyes were enormous as she blinked, twice, then cooed and wrinkled up her little button nose at Marc. Then she lost all interest in him and went back to her meal.

"She's incredible," he said.

"I know."

"I love her, too, Ginny."

Ginny felt tears flooding her eyes. She knew what he was offering—he would love not only her, but her daughter, as well. He was offering them everything he had to give, everything Ginny wanted for her baby.

She closed her eyes and savored the words. His love was something she would treasure. She would hold it in her heart and draw strength from it, because they had some difficult days ahead of them.

She knew there was no turning back now for her and Marc—no more trying to hide this relationship from anyone. There'd be hell to pay; he knew it as well as she did. But then, there would always be hell to pay, whenever she started seeing anyone. She couldn't believe it would be any easier on Joe's family six months from now or a year from now. And she didn't think Marc would wait, after the step they'd taken last night.

"Ginny?" He sounded worried now.

She kissed him, lightly, on the lips, feeling that little buzz of awareness flash between them, as it always did. Then she nuzzled her nose against the side of his face. "I'm right here," she said. And she wasn't going anywhere.

Ginny felt a shudder work its way through his body and knew he'd been as worried about this morning-after stuff as she. His arm came around her shoulders, and his other one reached out to Hannah, who was totally absorbed in her morning meal. Marc put his hand on Hannah's head, then her cheek. Soon one of her hands had latched on to his finger, and she held on for dear life.

"I couldn't love her any more if she was my own," he promised.

Ginny felt her tears overflow and spill down her cheeks. He seemed to know just what to say to tug at her heart. And she knew what else he was doing—staking his claim. Hannah was his now, as well.

"Everything's going to be all right, Ginny. I swear it will."

She busied herself trying to burp the baby, who was half-full and ready to play, now that she'd spotted Marc. Twisting her little body around so that she could give him a smile bright enough to light up a small city, Hannah gurgled and cooed and flirted with him shamelessly.

"Hannah, we're not done here," Ginny reminded her.

Hannah turned back to her mother, batted her baby blues, then turned back to Marc. But this is something new! she seemed to say. He's here!

"You're distracting her," Ginny said, and didn't add that she found him quite distracting herself, even as she settled Hannah against her other breast.

"Get used to it, ladies. I'm here for the duration."

Ginny should have objected to that, but the truth was, she was drawn to the idea. Having him here beside her, having him bring the baby to her in the middle of the night, then sit up with her while she fed Hannah. Having him stroke the baby's nearly nonexistent hair and say things that set her nerve endings on alert in that deep, husky, sleep-softened voice of his. She liked this whole idea a lot.

Oh, she had a million questions about what was going to happen come morning and what was going to happen the following night. Would it be a repeat of this night? Ginny trembled in anticipation.

Could it be so easy? Could she just reach out and grab all this happiness, despite the complications it would bring? It looked so easy, yet she knew their future together would not come without a price. Sooner or later, she would start paying.

She fed the baby in silence, with Marc's arm around her shoulders, his face against her cheek, as he watched. When Hannah was done, Marc took her and carried her back to her crib in the other room. When he came back, he stood in the center of the room for a minute, watching her, waiting.

He could heat her body with nothing but the look in his eyes. He could set her heart to pounding, make her mouth go dry, her palms itch to touch him. In the faint light in the room, she saw shadows and hollows, planes and rippling muscles, tension and need straining inside him. What was he waiting for now? What did he want from her?

Ginny swallowed hard and pulled back the covers on the other side of the bed, inviting him to take his place beside her.

He didn't move for a second, seeming to be frozen there, and then she saw the chinks in the armor. As he climbed into the bed beside her, she saw that his pulse was thundering in his neck. There was a fine sheen of perspiration on his chest, and his hand, when he reached for her, was trembling.

He turned to her, resting his weight on one elbow, using the other arm to pull her to him. "I don't think I've ever been so afraid of anything," he admitted.

And then Ginny remembered how much she trusted him, how much she admired him, how safe she'd always felt with him. This was Marc, and everything was going to be fine.

He took a handful of her hair and gave a gentle tug, which sent her head tilting back to meet his mouth. Ginny opened to him, waiting for that feeling to hit her all over again. Need, excitement, impatience—he brought out all that in her in an instant.

His hand abandoned her hair, to slide down the side of his shirt that she'd slipped on. Then his palm took the weight of one of her breasts. Her nipple puckered in response.

As he settled his lower body against hers, her legs parted eagerly, drawing him closer. Already the throbbing was building. Already she felt empty and achy. She cradled his arousal against her and started rocking gently against him.

"Ginny," he warned, dragging his mouth away from hers, "one night is never going to be enough."

The banging noise came first, again from somewhere far away. But Ginny was deliciously warm and relaxed, feeling as lazy as a cat on a hot summer day. She stretched, sighed, then felt a raspy hardness nuzzling against her neck, one she recognized as Marc's jaw.

Then the pounding started again.

Her eyes flew open. She turned and struggled to focus on the time on the clock, then turned back to see the sunshine projecting through the closed curtains.

"Marc?" She caught her breath for a second at the sight of him there, his hair tousled, his eyes closed, his skin a warm brown against the stark white sheet. She didn't want this night to end, but someone was giving them no choice. "Marc? It's almost nine, and someone's pounding on the door."

He came awake quickly, she noted. One moment he wa
lying flat on the bed, and the next he looked remarkabl
alert. He gave her a quick, hard kiss, then turned towar
the sound of someone banging on the door. In the nex
instant, he was scrambling into his clothes.

"Time to face the music, I guess." He looked sombe
at the thought. "Just so you know, I don't think it's any
one's business how we spent last night, and I'm not go
ing to volunteer anything. But I'm through denying it."

Ginny could accept that, but she held out little hop
that whoever was at the door wouldn't make some sort o
accusation about her and Marc.

"Can you handle this?" he asked.

She hesitated.

"Oh, hell, Ginny, you shouldn't have to explain your
self to these people, and it's unfair of me to put you in thi
position at all."

Outside the door, the pounding increased. Whoever wa
out there was going to wake Hannah any minute.

"Hey," Marc offered, "why don't you jump in th
shower? That'll buy you a few minutes, at least. I'll go se
what I can do to calm our visitor down."

Ginny pulled the sheet tighter against herself. "Than
you."

Marc leaned down in front of her face so that he coul
look her in the eye. "Remember something. Remember
love you."

"I will." And with that, she fled.

Ginny turned on the water full blast and let the hot stin
of the streams of water do its best to clear her head an
bring her fully awake. All sound was muffled from ou
side the bathroom. Hannah hadn't awakened yet, but sh
would any minute now. The pounding on the door ha

stopped, but she heard voices—angry voices from the direction of the living room.

So, it had begun. Someone knew about her and Marc. Before the day was over, everyone would. At best, she would be branded a traitor to her husband's memory. She didn't want to think about the worst end of the spectrum. Ginny had no idea how long she would have been expected to mourn Joe. She couldn't have said that she was done with that process even now. But in the eyes of the Reed family, her grief would seem fleeting, even disrespectful.

It wasn't fair, but then, Ginny knew life wasn't fair. Joe had told her long ago that the price of a big, loving family was having the whole clan know your business and feel entitled to comment upon it.

Ginny didn't want to lose the Reeds. She wanted Hannah to grow up with that family bond, but she'd taken an irrevocable step toward Marc last night. She couldn't back away from that now.

Before she knew it, the water had turned cold on her. Ginny shut it off, dried herself and found that Marc had pushed her suitcase into the bathroom. She dug through it until she came up with jeans and a shirt, then dressed hastily. As she scrubbed her teeth, the knot in her stomach grew to gigantic proportions.

Whatever was coming, she was going to face it, now. Thinking about it any longer would only make it worse. Ginny found the bedroom empty. In the living room she found Marc, his expression thunderous, as he faced off against Antonio Reed.

Ginny was surprised by that. She'd have thought Mama Reed herself would be here, or that she'd send Jimmy.

"Well, well, what have we here?" Antonio gave her an insolent look, one that managed to make her feel cheap and insulted, all at the same time.

Ginny held her head high and wished she didn't blush so easily. "What are you doing here?" she asked, ready to go on the offensive.

"I came to take you back to your family, where you belong."

He always had been an insolent boy, and he hadn't ever managed to outgrow that stage. "Antonio, don't you dare come in here and presume to tell me that you know where I belong or that you've decided to take me anywhere."

He dismissed her with a bitter stare. "You don't know this man, not the way you think you know him."

"Oh, really?" Ginny said.

"Do you know what he's been doing the past few days? Do you know who he's working for?"

Ginny couldn't say exactly what happened then. It was as if the temperature in the room had dropped ten degrees. Marc stood ramrod-straight, tension the only thing she could read in his expression. She thought he could have cheerfully knocked Antonio to the floor. And she must not have been as sure of Marc Dalton as she believed, because a first flicker of doubt ran through her mind.

What did Antonio mean? Did she know what Marc had been doing these past few days?

Of course, there was an answer to that—he'd been trying to find out what Joe had been involved in before he died, and he'd done that at Ginny's request. Surely that was what Antonio meant, and she couldn't allow him to question Marc's loyalty because of it.

She forced herself to face Antonio. "It's not what you think."

"It's not?" He looked incredulous. Then he had the nerve to laugh out loud. "Sugar, this man's got you snowed. One roll in the sack and you're willing to believe anything he says, but let me tell you—"

Marc grabbed Antonio by the front of his shirt and hauled the man around to face him. "Get out of my house. Now."

Antonio shoved Marc away from him. A good yard separated them now. Ginny could breathe again. Maybe they wouldn't come to blows after all.

"I'll go," Antonio told Marc. "But you should know— I drove by your house last night to have a little talk with you about Ginny. I saw O'Connor's car."

Marc didn't move then.

Antonio looked quite satisfied with himself when he turned to Ginny. "I'll wait outside for you to pack your things and get the baby."

"I'm not going anywhere with you," Ginny said.

"Sure you will." Antonio paused in the doorway. "As soon as you ask him what a good friend he's been to your husband, how loyal, how trustworthy."

"I don't think you heard me," Ginny said.

"And you didn't let me finish. Ask lover boy what he's been doing for internal affairs."

Antonio slammed the door behind him as he left. The sound reverberated through the house. Ginny was watching the door, with Marc to her left and slightly behind her, so she couldn't see him. She wasn't sure she wanted to see him, not yet.

She had to think for a minute first.

Internal affairs? The people who thought her husband was a dirty cop? Cautiously, a sickening feeling racing through her, she turned to Marc. "This internal affairs investigation didn't start yesterday with the knife, did it?"

"No."

Ginny nodded. "And you knew about it."

He nodded.

She watched him closely, her longtime friend, her husband's partner, now her lover. She fought the doubts that threatened to overtake her. She knew the kind of person Marc was. If she could trust anyone on this earth, it was Marc. She'd stake her life on that. So why did she suddenly feel so cold?

"Why didn't you tell me?" she asked. "Didn't you think I had a right to know?"

He flinched. "Ginny, I knew how much it would hurt you."

She nodded. "And you and the rest of the family and probably the rest of the world are in on some conspiracy to keep anything from upsetting me."

"I haven't made any kind of deal with the Reeds. And as far as I know, until yesterday, no one in the family had any idea about the investigation. If they did, they weren't talking about it."

Marc moved to take her hand, but she jerked away from him.

She squeezed her eyes closed. When she opened them again, tears overflowed and ran down her cheeks. Through bleary eyes, she saw Marc. The expression on his face was painful just to watch.

Antonio's accusations were sinking in, her thoughts managing to form some semicoherent pattern inside her head. "You knew about this investigation all along? And you didn't say anything to me?"

"I didn't know anything for sure until the day of Hannah's baptism."

And then there was nothing left but the hardest question of all.

"You didn't... Marc, you're not a part of this. Tell me you're not investigating Joe."

He didn't have to answer her. The expression on his face said it all. She hadn't seen him looking this bleak since he'd come to tell her Joe was dead.

As she had that day, Ginny found the whole thing so hard to take in. She stood there for what might have been forever, what might have been mere seconds, and once again watched her whole world tilt on its axis because of something this man had told her.

Her mind kept flashing back to the night they'd spent together, to the way she'd given herself to him, the life she'd envisioned living with him and with Hannah.

A bitter taste rose up in her mouth, and she almost gagged. "Why?"

"It's not what you think," he said.

Ginny almost laughed. "That's what I've been telling Joe's family about you and me. *It's not what you think.* But then, we both know that it was. It was exactly what they thought. God, what a fool I've been."

"No!" He took her by the arms and turned her to face him. "No!"

Ginny jerked away and walked across the room before turning to face him again as the enormity of his deception became clear.

"You said you'd help me. You promised. And I trusted you. I've spent the past two weeks catching all sorts of hell from Joe's family because of you, and I've defended you to them all. I said—" Ginny's voice broke on the words, and she had to struggle to continue. "I told them I trusted you. What a joke that turned out to be."

"Ginny..." he began.

"It's true. I came to you. I asked you for help. I told you I thought my husband was leaving me for another woman—that I thought this woman was the reason he was acting so strangely before he died—and you just let me. You just listened to me, and then . . . you took notes and ran back to headquarters to tell them what you'd gotten out of me."

She nearly fell to her knees when he didn't deny it. This was worse, so much worse, than anything she'd imagined.

"That was your assignment, wasn't it? To see what you could get out of me? And I played right into your hands. Right into your arms." She glanced back toward the room off to the left, bitterness eating away at her now. "Right into your bed."

"It wasn't like that, and you know it."

"I don't know anything right now, except that I trusted you and you lied to me. Isn't that the way it was?"

Again Marc said nothing. He stood there, frozen, in the middle of the room. The clock on the mantel ticked off the seconds, and Ginny was so mad she was shaking, so hurt she thought her heart was going to come apart inside her.

How could she have been so wrong? How?

Ginny had no idea where she was going or who she could trust now. And then she remembered—Antonio was waiting for her outside.

Her face burned at the idea of facing him or any of the family right now. But it would get her out of Marc's house, and that idea was incredibly appealing. Given a choice between facing the Reeds and staying here with him, she decided to swallow her pride and get in the car with Antonio.

She turned and saw Marc coming toward her. Ginny held up her hands and backed away, not wanting him within touching distance, not wanting to think of what it did to her when he touched her.

"I know how it sounds—" he began.

"No." She cut him off. "Not how it sounds. How it is. I haven't heard you deny it. I'm sure you would if you could."

"Ginny, I love you."

"Ohhh!" She cried out, it hurt so badly. "Don't say that. Please, don't say that. Don't try to tell me you were lying to me about this, but you really meant it when you said you loved me. Don't even try to convince me of that."

"All right. I won't."

Ginny took a deep breath. She ran a hand over her face, wiping away the remainder of her tears. It was time to move, time to get away from him. "I'm going to get my suitcases and my daughter, and I'm leaving."

She turned and headed for the bathroom. When she'd stuffed her things in her case and zipped it, she found him waiting at the door, his hand reaching out to take the case from her. Ginny flinched as her hand brushed against his when she gave it to him, and she would have sworn her reaction brought him some physical pain, as well.

But she couldn't afford to think about what he was feeling, or whether he felt anything at all.

She went to the room Hannah was using, found that Marc had already carried out her suitcase, leaving only the baby, who was finally starting to stir. Ginny caught Hannah close, and the baby snuggled against her, so warm, so soft, such a welcome weight in her arms.

"Oh, Hannah," she said, her composure starting to crack.

Ginny bit back bitter tears, gathered up Hannah's favorite blanket and decided to leave the portable crib. She couldn't face the time it would take to break it down and get it back in its case. She would send someone for it later.

Marc was standing by the back door when she walked down the hall and into the kitchen. He stared at her, his eyes dark, his jawline so tight it might have been carved of stone.

Hannah looked up and smiled at him. She reached out to him, and that was nearly Ginny's undoing. Marc leaned over the baby and gave her a quick kiss on the forehead. Ginny turned away. She pushed Hannah's head down against her chest and headed for the door.

Marc's hand shot out to stop her, to hold her in place when he told her, "This isn't over."

Ginny jerked her arm away from his hand. "Don't you dare try to tell me this meant something to you, that meant something to you."

He looked as if he'd been begging for the invitation to do just that, and Ginny worried about what she'd done, what she'd started here, when she was so close to escaping.

"You think about it," he said. "You think about the years you've known me. Do you honestly believe I'm the kind of person who would use anybody like that?"

Ginny was mad enough to want to hurt him deliberately. "Isn't that what you did?"

Chapter 15

Marc wanted to go after Ginny, but he fought the urge. Even if he caught up with her now, he didn't think she was ready to listen to his explanation. He had to believe that someday he could explain and she would listen.

Still, he felt sick inside. He felt as if every dream he'd ever had had just walked out his door. How could he have gotten one glorious night with her, only to lose her for good in the morning?

He wouldn't let that happen.

He'd have loved to believe this wasn't his fault but the truth was painfully clear. He could have been honest with her from the start. Even if knowing about the investigation would have hurt her in the beginning, he could see now that she'd been hurt more by being kept in the dark.

He'd just have to find a way to make her forgive him. And he would never lie to her about anything again.

Marc brushed a hand through his hair, then looked around his empty house. What was he going to do now?

Let her calm down? Go looking for her later? Run through the things he had to say to her? Maybe if he did that about a dozen times, he could get it straight.

Still, he felt uneasy about letting her out of his sight. Something in his gut told him it was a mistake.

He decided to make some coffee, hoping that would help wake him up. While it was brewing, he showered and dressed. Then he sat at his kitchen table and tried to think.

Someone wanted Joe Reed to look guilty. Someone wanted to link him to Renata Leone's murder.

If someone was trying to frame Joe, did that mean Ginny was in danger, as well? If he thought she was, he wouldn't let her out of his sight again until this was resolved, no matter how angry that made Ginny. His first priority had to be her and Hannah's safety.

As Marc saw it, he had only one option. He had to solve this case, now, before anyone else got hurt.

And maybe then he could convince Ginny to give him another chance.

He looked around the room, thinking about where he could start, what he had missed, and his gaze hit on the little pad of paper he kept by the phone so that he could jot down numbers and messages. A little red notebook—just like Joe's.

In the confusion and shock over the knife found in Joe's basement, he'd totally forgotten about the notebook.

He went into his bedroom and found that notebook. Impatiently he started going through it. It was a fight to force himself to move slowly, methodically, carefully. He understood how Joe had thought. He could read Joe's shorthand of numbers and initials fairly well. After all, Joe had taught him to keep a notebook just like this when Marc joined the force.

Marc also knew many of Joe's sources. Many had turned to Marc after Joe's death. Forty-five minutes after he started working his way through the notebook, he was frustrated and even more impatient than before.

He made a quick call to Barbara, learned that Ginny wasn't there yet, then tried his best to tell Barbara as little as possible. "Just have her call me the minute she comes in, okay? Or if she won't call me, you call. Just to tell me she's there and she's safe."

"What's going on?" Barbara asked.

"We had a misunderstanding." He didn't plan to elaborate on that at all.

Barbara hesitated. She seemed to read everything he'd left unsaid into that comment. "Marc, don't you hurt her," she added.

"Aw, dammit, I already have."

"Marc—"

"No." He cut her off. "I can't get into this right now. I have too many other things to take care of. Barbara, this is important. Promise me—if Ginny comes in, don't let her leave. I'll be over as soon as you call me."

It was a half hour later that Marc thought to count the pages in the notebook. The cover promised one hundred pages. The notebook yielded only ninety-five. Marc thought back. He didn't think he remembered ever seeing Joe tear a page out of one of these notebooks. He'd kept business cards instead, and he'd always jotted down notes on the back of those.

A quick check of the two preceding notebooks of Joe's—which he'd taken from the house days before—showed that each still had a hundred pages. If Joe hadn't torn out those five missing pages, someone else had.

His heart pounding, Marc searched the house until he came up with a pencil and some thin, plain paper. He placed the paper over the last sheet in Joe's notebook and rubbed the lead gently across it. Nothing showed until he was eighteen pages from the back. Then he caught the faint impression of a series of numbers that didn't appear on that page. They must have come from the previous page—one of the five that were missing from the notebook.

The impression was faint, but when he was done, Marc was staring at what looked like the initial *A,* maybe *7th* for a street name, and Joe's version of a date, which he'd always written to look like a phone number. The date was the last five or six digits. In this case, it looked like April 28 of the previous year, approximately a month before Joe had been killed.

A.

Who was *A?*

Normally Joe would have included two initials, for both a first and a last name. Of course there had been times when Joe didn't have the last name of a source or a suspect. That could be the reason. But Marc didn't know of any source of Joe's whose name began with an *A.*

He couldn't think of any cases, any suspects, where they'd only had a single name that started with an *A.*

Why else would Joe use only one initial? Maybe if that last initial was an *R?* As in Reed?

Antonio Reed?

Marc's blood ran cold at the thought.

To be sure, he ran through the list of cousins he could remember, then the immediate family. There was no one else whose name started with an *A.*

And Antonio was a hothead. He'd been furious that Ginny was becoming involved with Marc. Maybe because it frightened him? Maybe because he thought Marc knew more than he should about Joe's death?

Antonio had been with Ginny when she went through the house this morning. He'd been there when she found the notebook. He would have had time to plant it, to make sure she found it.

And Antonio had told Ginny about Marc's involvement in the internal affairs investigation. How had he known that? Had he simply driven by the house and spotted O'Connor as he'd said? Or had he been watching Marc? Following him—because he was suspicious of what Marc had been doing?

Everything would fall into place if the culprit was a member of the family. It would explain a lot about the last few months of Joe's life. If he'd found out his cousin was involved with those dirty cops, Joe might have kept quiet about it at first. Or maybe it had just taken him some time to figure out exactly what was going on. Maybe he'd had nothing but suspicions. He wouldn't have said anything to anyone without proof.

Marc could see Joe feeling enough loyalty to the family that he would try his best to help his cousin. But what if his cousin was breaking the law? Would Joe help him then?

Maybe.

Marc shook his head. Joe must not have been sure; he hadn't had any hard evidence. That was what had gotten Joe caught in the middle of a gunfight. He'd followed Antonio to that apartment building to see what his cousin was up to.

That would explain why Joe hadn't told Marc where he was going.

Yes, the more Marc thought about it, the more it all fit.

Antonio Reed had to be the one. And Marc had just let Ginny and Hannah leave with him.

Marc grabbed his gun and was out the door in seconds, headed for his car. Gut instinct told him that he had no time to lose. His head told him that Antonio wouldn't hurt Ginny or the baby. His heart told him he couldn't take that risk—that he had to find them, now.

Using his car phone, he first called Mama Reed, then Barbara. Mama Reed's line was busy. Either that or she'd taken the phone off the hook because the press had gotten wind of the whole mess with Joe and the knife. Barbara didn't answer the phone, Jimmy did, and he wasn't in the mood to be friendly. He first demanded to know where Ginny was and where she had been, then asked what the hell Marc knew about this whole investigation.

Marc barely got a word in edgewise, but finally found out that Antonio still lived about six blocks away, in the same apartment he'd had for the past two years. That was good. Marc knew the place. He cut Jimmy off and finally got him to promise that at the very least, if Ginny came back, he would keep her there. Marc decided not to tell Jimmy about Antonio yet, mostly because he didn't think Jimmy would believe him. And Marc didn't have time to argue. Instead he raced toward Antonio's apartment.

Antonio drove a black sports car that wasn't in the parking lot when Marc arrived. Getting out of the car, Marc ran to the apartment's door and pounded anyway. Antonio's girlfriend, Sharon, opened the door just as far as the chain would allow.

"Where's Antonio?" he demanded.

"Out," she replied curtly.

"Out where?"

"I don't know. He doesn't exactly report in to me, if you know what I mean."

She turned slightly to the left when she said it, and Marc thought he saw some puffiness around her eye. The light wasn't that good, but he thought she might have a cut lip, as well.

"Sharon, you know who I am. I'm his cousin Joey's ex-partner, and I want you to open this door. Now."

"I told you, he's not here." She went to slam the door, but Marc stuck his foot in the opening.

"If you don't open it, now, I'm going to break it down," he said, feeling out of control enough to do just that.

She didn't respond. Marc shouldered the obviously cheap door, testing the strength of it. Sharon screamed. Across the hall, a door opened, and a startled woman shook a baseball bat at him and threatened to call the cops on him if he didn't leave the poor girl in that apartment alone.

"Lady, I am a cop." Marc flipped open the leather case he carried his shield in.

"And that's supposed to make me feel better? That little creep who lives there's a cop, too. Well, let me tell you, you're not going to beat that girl the way he does. Nobody's going to beat that girl anymore and get away with it."

The woman slammed the door. No doubt she was going to call 911, and the place would be crawling with cops any minute. Marc didn't see that he had any time to waste. He kicked in the door.

Sharon, huddled against the back wall of the living room, screamed as the door gave way and Marc came inside. He flicked on the overhead light and saw the swelling around her eye now, the bruising, the lip split at the corners.

Well, how about that? Antonio Reed beat his girlfriend. What else did he do?

Marc, worried about really frightening the girl, now that he could see her condition, held up both hands in front of him in an effort to reassure her. "I'm not going to hurt you," he said. "All I want to know is where Antonio is."

"I don't know, honest. He left this morning, about an hour and a half ago, and he didn't say where he was going."

"He has Ginny. And the baby." Marc hoped that would mean something to the girl.

It did. She started to cry.

Aw, dammit, Marc thought. Antonio would hurt Ginny, too, just as he'd hurt this girl, if he got the chance. It was up to Marc to see that Antonio didn't get that chance.

"You know what he's been doing, don't you?" He pressed forward, out of options, out of time. "You know he's involved with these cops coming to trial. You know he was likely the cause of Joe's death."

The girl nodded. "But he didn't mean for Joey to get hurt. He never meant for anything like that to happen."

"Yeah, funny how things like that happen. He just wanted a little extra money. Maybe some drugs. And somebody ends up getting shot. He can tell that to the judge. I'm sure they'll take into account that Antonio never meant for his cousin to get killed."

Sharon was sobbing now. Marc heard the faint whine of the sirens in the distance, and knew he had to move. He wasn't in the mood to try to explain this situation and wait for his fellow officers to believe him and help him. He had to find Ginny—now.

"Where would he go?" he demanded. "He has Ginny and the baby. Where would he take them? Where would he hide?"

"I don't know," she sobbed.

"Think," Marc urged. "Where would he take them?"

Finally Sharon stopped crying and wiped her tears. "I don't know. Maybe back to Joey's house?"

"Back there? He was there before, right? He's the one who broke in the other night?"

Sharon started to cry again. "It was my fault," she said.

"Your fault?"

She nodded. "I was supposed to take some stuff and put it in the house, and then take some notebooks at the same time, while everybody was at the baseball game and cookout. It was supposed to be easy. Antonio gave me the key and told me not to come back until I got the job done. But the key didn't work, so I went in through the basement window, because . . . I was scared that if I didn't do what he said he'd come after me again."

"Go on," Marc said.

"I couldn't find the notebooks. They weren't where Antonio said they'd be, so I started looking around for them, and the more scared I got, the sloppier the search. Pretty soon, I'd made a real mess. And when I called Antonio and told him what I'd done, he kind of lost his temper."

"So he finished the job himself? Then beat you because the locks had been changed and the key didn't fit and the notebooks were gone?"

Sharon hesitated. "He has a bad temper."

The cuts and bruises on her face said that all too well. "So he had the knife and the notebook? That's what he gave you to put in the house?"

"Yes."

As he saw it, Antonio had been involved all along. When Renata Leone was killed, Antonio got worried. And then Joe was killed and everything must have been really crazy. Somehow, Antonio got hold of the knife Morris had used to kill Renata and kept it, maybe hoping it would give him some sort of leverage over Morris, who could spill his guts at any time. And then Antonio must have gotten really scared when internal affairs started investigating Joe. He must have been desperate to convince internal affairs that Joe was the dirty cop, maybe even one who was somehow involved in Renata's murder. Antonio must have hoped their investigation would stop right there with Joe, that it would never lead to the real dirty cop—Antonio.

"Look," Marc said, "I don't have much time. Why would Antonio go back to Joe's house?"

"I don't know. He doesn't tell me anything and I don't ask. But there was something he couldn't find the other night."

"What?"

"I don't know. He's not thinking straight right now. He's crazy."

Marc turned toward the door. The sirens were close now, and he debated what he should do. If he waited, he could go in with backup. But how long would it take him to convince the officer who responded to break into a former officer's house—if necessary—to catch another officer Marc thought was a crooked cop?

That was the kind of problem that took some explaining, and one thing Marc didn't have was time. Ginny and

Hannah were out there somewhere, and he had to find them. He turned around and left.

Marc raced to Ginny's house, driving in through the alley and parking three houses away. He drew his gun and carefully made his way down the alley. Antonio's car was in back of the house.

He crept up onto the porch and tried the back door, found it locked. Then he crept around to the sun room on the left side of the house and looked through the windows. Ginny was there, in the middle of the living room, sitting on the sofa. He didn't see Hannah anywhere, but Antonio was pacing the floor behind Ginny. Marc waited until he got a look at Antonio's hands. Both were empty. There was no weapon in sight.

Marc didn't think there was anything to do but go inside. He wasn't going to leave Ginny and Hannah in there a minute longer than he had to. Maybe Antonio wasn't as far gone as he feared, Marc told himself. Maybe he would give up without a fight.

Marc took a few moments to calm down. A cool head was what kept a cop alive. Unfortunately, all he could think about was keeping Ginny and the baby safe.

Marc held the gun in his hand, which was down at his side and behind his right hip. With his left hand, he knocked on the back door.

No response.

He knocked again, louder and sharper. "Ginny? I know you're in there, and I'm not leaving until you and I have a chance to talk."

Again, no response.

Marc swore. He thought about the dead bolts that had been installed a few days before, looked at the old and solid wooden door, and knew he wasn't going through this door as easily as he had the cheap one at Antonio's apartment.

He rapped on the door one more time and called out to Ginny.

Finally the door opened. Ginny stood in front of him, her right side hugging the door and her body blocking his way, so that he couldn't see much of anything behind her.

Willing himself to be calm, to keep thinking, he looked her over and was relieved to find no cuts or bruises on her face. But she looked terrified. Her eyes were big and round and wet from recent tears. She was trembling, and she was begging him with those eyes—begging him to do something.

What?

"I don't have anything to say to you," she said, slowly and carefully. "Do you understand?"

Perfectly. Antonio had her scared half to death.

Marc nodded. "Where's Hannah?" he mouthed to her.

Ginny glanced off to the right. Hannah must be upstairs. Much as he'd have loved to grab Ginny and pull her through the doorway, he couldn't. He'd never get Ginny to leave this house without her daughter. It wasn't even worth trying.

"Marc, please," she said, her voice shaky now. "You have to leave. Now."

"Not until you talk to me," he said, for Antonio's benefit. To her, he whispered. "Does he have a gun?"

She nodded. It took everything he had in him not to haul her into his arms and drag her out of here. But Antonio might be right behind the door.

All it took was a fraction of a second, he reminded himself, one bullet in the wrong spot, and it was all over.

"On you? Now?" Marc mouthed.

"No," Ginny said aloud. She stumbled for a minute, then continued when she remembered the role they were playing. "I've said all I have to say to you. Now go away."

Her voice, already strained, grew higher and tighter, as if she were in pain. Marc's guess was that Antonio was right beside her.

He was out of time. She was going to close the door, and then he'd have no choice but to break in somehow. He wouldn't get a better opportunity than this. He took one last look at her beautiful, tearstained face, then closed his eyes, willing himself once again to think. His whole future was on the line here. Without Ginny and Hannah, what would he have? And yet he couldn't afford to hesitate.

To Ginny, he merely nodded and tried not to let his fear show.

"Go away," she said. "Please."

"Go left, on three," he mouthed to her.

"No!" Ginny screamed.

Marc shouldered his way past her, pushing her to his right, and shoving against the door with all his might, following that up with his gun, drawn and pointing toward the space behind the door.

The door swung all the way back and banged against the back wall, the momentum pushing it back toward him. Marc swore. Antonio wasn't behind the damned door. Marc's gun was aiming at nothing but thin air.

Behind him, Hannah started screaming. He could hear it once the roaring in his ears subsided. Hannah was screaming, and then Marc knew. The hairs on the back of his neck stood on end. Before he ever turned around, he knew there was a gun pointing right at his back. Antonio's gun.

"Slowly," Antonio warned.

Marc started to move, cautiously this time, damning himself with each second it took to face the man giving the orders now.

Antonio had his service revolver in his right hand, Hannah in his left.

Marc swore again.

"Now, close the door," Antonio ordered. "Slowly."

Marc did so, then saw Ginny on her knees. He went to help her, but Antonio objected.

"The gun!" he said, having to yell to be heard over Hannah's frightened cries. "Unload it and put the bullets on the table!"

Marc did that, too, fuming as he moved and wishing he'd waited for the officers responding to the 911 call from Antonio's apartment.

"Now the gun," Antonio said. "Put it on the top of the refrigerator, behind you."

Marc gave up his weapon, then moved over to Ginny and offered her his hand. He wasn't sure she would take it, considering what he'd done to her in the past two hours, but she did.

Her trembling hand closed around his. Her eyes met his, and he couldn't read the emotions he found there. Did she hate him? For botching this so badly? Or for everything? She might well hate him forever after this.

Ginny got to her feet, and Marc pulled her to his side. Thankfully, she didn't fight him on that. He held her there, the feel of her beside him calming him now.

Poor Hannah, scared by the noise and the sudden movement, was still screaming.

"Give Ginny the baby," Marc said.

Antonio shook his head.

"You've got the gun," Marc argued. "You don't need her. And you may have done a lot of terrible things, but you're not going to hurt Joe's baby. It's bad enough that you got him killed.''

Antonio could have spit fire, from the look on his face. ''I did not get Joey killed.''

''Yeah, right,'' Marc said.

Ginny gasped. ''What? He's the reason Joe died?''

''He's the reason Joe was in front of that building that day.''

''Antonio?'' she asked.

''I didn't do anything to Joey. Joey did that to himself, sticking his nose in where it didn't belong.''

''Oh, my God,'' Ginny said, sagging against Marc's side.

Marc held her tightly and tried not to think about the last time he had her in his arms. They would have a future together. He vowed to get them out of this mess. ''I love you, Ginny,'' he said, his lips against her hair.

And he would make it up to her for hurting her this morning. He had to believe he'd have that chance someday.

Grimly he turned back to Antonio and little Hannah, who was howling as never before. ''Give Ginny the baby,'' he repeated, ''otherwise you're going to have to figure out how to get out of this thing with Hannah screaming in your ear.''

Antonio was obviously rattled by all the noise, yet he still resisted. ''I don't have to figure anything out. I'm holding all the cards.''

''Maybe, for now, but if you want to get out of here, you'd better go now. You don't think I'd come into this house without backup, do you?''

It was a calculated risk. If Antonio knew how crazy Marc was about Ginny and Hannah, he'd know that Marc hadn't waited. But Marc suspected Antonio didn't care about anyone except himself. So he wouldn't understand what had propelled Marc into this house by himself, despite the risks.

"You're lying," Antonio said.

"Do you want to take that chance? Because I don't. I don't want the hostage-rescue team breaking into this house with you and that gun and Ginny's baby inside."

"You're bluffing," Antonio insisted.

"Give her the baby, and take me. My patrol car's in the alley, and there's a police radio in it. Between the car, the radio and me, you can get out of town."

Marc would gladly go and take his chances with Antonio, if it meant Ginny and the baby would be safe.

"Nobody's coming after me," Antonio insisted, though he clearly wasn't convinced. And Hannah seemed to be getting to him. She was squirming now, making her hard to hang on to with only one hand.

"Please," Ginny said. "Please don't hurt my baby."

"Take me," Marc said, "and let's go, while you can still get out of here."

Antonio wavered. From somewhere in the distance came the faint wail of a siren, and the sound had the three of them catching their breaths.

"I'll be damned," Antonio said.

"Yes, you will. Give her the baby, and let's go."

"All right," he said, motioning to Ginny. "Come and get her before she breaks my damned eardrums."

Ginny hesitated, glancing at Marc.

"Go ahead," he said, squeezing her to him for a quick second. "I'll be fine. After all, I still have a lot of explaining to do."

A flicker of pain passed through her eyes, and then she took a deep breath and turned back toward her daughter.

"Slowly," Marc urged her, and he held his breath the whole time it took her to approach Antonio and take Hannah from his arms.

He felt much better once Hannah was in her mother's arms. Felt better still when Ginny stepped back and to the right, out of the line of fire.

The sirens were still coming closer. Marc didn't have much time. He wanted Antonio well away from Ginny and the baby before anyone else arrived on the scene.

"We've got to go, if we're going," Marc said.

Antonio was scared. The sirens had done that much, at least. He turned to Ginny. "I never meant for anything to happen to Joey," he said. "Never. You've got to understand that. You've got to make the family understand that."

Ginny looked as if she could cheerfully spit on Antonio, but she said nothing. She just held her baby close and tried to soothe her.

"We have to go," Marc said, just beginning to think about how he was going to get away from this crazy kid himself.

"Ginny?" Antonio said. "You have to tell them. I never meant for that to happen."

"I wouldn't defend you to the devil himself," she said.

Antonio paled. Mama Reed was a churchgoer, like the entire family. Clearly, someone had once painted a vivid picture of hell for Antonio.

"He thought I was going to get killed out there," Antonio confessed. "Morris and I argued—about taking out Renata Leone's kid—and Morris had a gun. All Joey saw was someone out there on the streets that day with a gun pointed at me, and he thought I was as good as dead. He didn't know . . . at least he wasn't sure I was working with them. He screamed a warning to me and raised his gun.

None of us had spotted the FBI agents yet. One of them must have pulled a gun, and Joe fired at the agent. While Joe was doing that, Morris shot him. And then all hell broke loose.''

Ginny stared him down from a face that was as pale as parchment paper, but she said nothing.

Marc listened to the sirens and urged Antonio, ''We have to go now.''

Antonio still hesitated. He turned back to Ginny. ''I didn't want to bring the knife back here, but Morris has a lot of friends. He was putting pressure on me. He was going to make sure that if he ended up in prison, I would, too. He thought implicating Joe in Renata Leone's murder was his only chance.''

''You're going to prison real soon, Antonio, if you don't get the hell out of here, now,'' Marc said insistently.

Antonio gave in. He waved his gun toward the door. Marc took one last look at Ginny and the baby in her arms, then turned and walked out the door.

He refused to tell her goodbye.

This was not goodbye.

Chapter 16

A shocked Ginny sank into a kitchen chair, her baby in her arms. This had been the worst experience of her life.

It was worse than the day Joe died, because today she'd honestly feared for her daughter's safety. Hannah squirmed against her now, trying to burrow even closer to her mother, and she was still trembling from her crying fit.

"Shhhh," Ginny whispered, trying to soothe Hannah by rocking back and forth, the way she did at night, when it was time for Hannah to go to sleep.

Ginny thought back to how strange Antonio had been acting from the moment she got into the car with him. But Ginny was so upset by what Marc had told her that she hadn't thought much of Antonio's agitated state.

After Antonio drove them back to her house, he'd begun questioning her about Joe—the last few months of his life, the things he'd told Ginny, the kinds of cases he'd been working on, the kind of notes he'd kept and the hiding places he'd used.

At first, Ginny had been sure Antonio thought Joe had actually been involved in that woman's murder, that the knife had been in their basement for a reason. She'd thought Antonio just wanted to know what Marc had found and what he believed Joe had done.

But the more they talked and the more Ginny thought about it, the more she'd been convinced—Antonio didn't think Joe had done anything wrong.

And then it had all come together here in the kitchen. When Marc showed up at the door, Antonio had grabbed Hannah from her and pulled out his revolver, then told Ginny she'd better get rid of Marc, or else.

Now she knew Antonio wasn't worried about evidence against Joe; he was concerned that Marc had found the same evidence Joe had—linking Antonio to the whole mess.

Antonio was the one involved with those crooked cops. He was the reason Joe had been at that apartment building that day, the reason Joe had been killed.

Hannah rubbed her nose and her wet face against her mother's shoulder, then laid her cheek against Ginny's neck and started sucking on the side of her hand. She'd calmed down now, and her breath was coming in big, long, uneven gulps.

"Oh, my baby," Ginny said, still seeing Antonio with one hand around her daughter and one hand around his gun.

She would still be there if Marc hadn't gotten Hannah away from Antonio, then gotten him out of the house.

Marc had forced his way in here with nothing but guts, effort and his own gun. He had to have known what he was facing, because he'd somehow figured out that Antonio was the key to this whole bewildering mess.

Yet he hadn't hesitated, either in getting inside or in getting Antonio out.

He'd willingly traded his own safety for hers and Hannah's. The enormity of that sacrifice stunned her.

She was still struggling with her anger and hurt over the fact that he'd betrayed her. But she couldn't ignore what he'd just done in this room, either.

Frozen to her spot, to the chair, six feet from the nearest window, Ginny tried to think about what to do next. The sirens were growing closer. Surely the police were coming here. If not, she had to call. She had to get someone to help Marc, to get him away from Antonio.

On shaky legs, Ginny rose and deposited Hannah in the living room playpen. Then she walked cautiously over to the kitchen window.

She was scared to look out that window. She was scared to open the door, scared of what she would find outside.

Thinking back, she realized she hadn't heard a car start, hadn't heard anyone drive away.

Were they still out there? Or had she simply been so caught up in her own chaotic thoughts that she hadn't paid any attention to the sound of the car?

Cursing herself and her cowardice, Ginny peeled back the curtains. Antonio's sports car was still in the driveway. Marc's car was nowhere to be seen. Her hands shaking, Ginny struggled to pick up the phone receiver and dial 911. It took a while for her to make the dispatcher understand all that had happened, and if there were units on the way to Ginny's house, the dispatcher didn't have any record of it.

Still, the sirens were coming. Not five seconds later, a police car halted in front of her house. Despite the dispatcher's pleas for Ginny to remain on the line, she dropped the phone and headed for the front door. She opened it as two officers, their guns drawn, reached her front door.

"It's all right," she told them. "Antonio's gone."

And then she started to cry.

It wasn't all right. Marc was gone, too, and Antonio probably had a gun pointed straight at him.

"Mrs. Reed?" The man on the right flashed a badge, then took her by the arm as two other police cars screeched to a halt in front of the house. "I'm Detective O'Connor, internal affairs. This is Detective Williams. Are you all right?"

Ginny nodded.

"Where's Officer Antonio Reed?"

"You know, don't you?" Ginny asked.

"That he's the one we're looking for? Yes, ma'am, think we have the whole thing figured out now."

Good. That was good. They knew, and they could help.

"Mrs. Reed? Where's Officer Reed? And Detective Dalton?"

"They're gone," she said, struggling to hold herself together. "Antonio had a gun. He had my daughter...and his gun...and Marc convinced him to let Hannah and me go. Antonio took Marc instead."

"Where are they?"

Ginny turned to the back of the house. Where had they gone? Surely they couldn't have gotten far. "Marc said his car was in back, but I didn't see it."

"Circle the back," O'Connor told two officers behind him, then turned back to Ginny. "That would be his police vehicle?"

"Yes."

"How long ago?"

"I don't..." Ginny couldn't begin to tell him that. She had no perception of time right now. "I don't know."

And then, from the back of the house and to the right, she heard shouts, and a popping sound that seemed to cut right through her. Ginny's knees buckled. Her stomach churned. One of the officers grabbed her and held her upright. The other was motioning for the other men to follow him to the side of the house. She saw weapons come out, saw them moving cautiously but quickly around the side of her house, before a second officer stepped up to the front door and insisted she get inside the house.

Officer Williams pulled a radio from his pocket and started calling in information in the shorthand of police code.

Ginny knew the codes all too well, from the days when she'd sat in her house late at night, worrying about Joe and listening to the police scanner. Still, she was working hard to follow the conversation that exploded on the radio channel.

And then she heard it—the call that strikes terror in the heart of every policeman's wife, the call that must have gone out that day she lost Joe.

Shots fired.

Officer down.

Ginny took off running for the back of the house. One of the officers took off after her. He was yelling for her to stop, but she wouldn't. She couldn't.

Marc was back there, and she had to get to him.

The kitchen door stopped her. By the time she tore it open, the officer had caught up with her and held her back.

"You can't go out there yet," he insisted.

"I'm going."

"Give me a second, okay? Let me talk to my guys on the radio."

Ginny hesitated, as did the man.

"Promise me you won't go running out there when I pick up my radio."

"Oh, God." She nodded and stared off into the yard. There were policemen running off to the left, more sirens screaming and the call over the radio still echoed through her head.

She heard Marc's voice calling her name the night before, when they'd been in his bed, heard him tell her that he loved her, that he wasn't going to let her go now.

Don't let go, she thought.

"Mrs. Reed?"

She turned to the man who still held on to her arm. "The scene's secure, and you can go back there, but..."

"What?"

"They're both injured, and—"

Ginny didn't wait to hear anything more. "Somebody stay with my baby," she said, then jerked her arm free and took off.

A knot of officers stood to the left of the hedges that bordered Ginny's property. They were all bigger than she was, all taller, and she had to fight her way through to see a thing. And when she did, she saw a pair of legs, clad in blue jeans, the upper body and the head obscured by the officers bending over to work to save the man.

She saw blood on the ground.

"Ginny?"

The voice was faint, not calling to her, just saying her name—maybe in surprise?

She turned so fast, her head started to spin. Another man was leaning heavily against the hood of the car. He had his back to her and was surrounded by two other officers.

Ginny blinked back tears to clear her vision as he turned, searching the crowd. She saw those short, tight curls on his head, saw blood coming through a piece of white cloth tied around his left arm.

And the next thing she knew, she was in his arms.

"Oh, Marc," she said, fighting for breath as one of his arms came around her and held her in a crushing hold. "I heard the shot, I heard the call go out on the radio. . ."

He kissed her forehead, then brought his lips down on hers for a hard, quick kiss. Beneath her hands, his heart skipped a beat, and some of the tension in her gave way.

Ginny eased herself away from him just a little, just enough that she could see him. She ran a hand over a nasty-looking bruise on his forehead, a cut at the corner of his mouth that had a trickle of blood trailing away from it.

Her hand lingered on his cheek, and then she felt his lips press a kiss against her palm.

She shifted against him, bumping into his left arm and sending a grimace of pain across his face.

"I'm sorry."

She'd been so anxious to take inventory of the rest of him that she'd forgotten about the arm. She turned to examine it and caught her breath. The wound was obviously high on his left arm, somewhere in that muscle she was so fond of, and there was more blood than she'd first realized.

Ginny put her hand over the now blood-soaked cloth that someone had wrapped around the wound. "What in the world are you doing on your feet?"

"Just what I've been trying to find out," said a man to her left, a man she recognized from the precinct house. "Come on. I want you lying on the ground and that arm up in the air."

The man took hold of Marc and helped him to the ground, where someone had spread a blanket. Ginny knelt beside him, covered him with the other half of the blanket and held the arm in the air to help stanch the flow of blood and put as much pressure on the wound as he could stand.

He looked a little dazed now—no doubt the adrenaline slowing down, the blood loss finally catching up with him—but he was intent on talking to her.

''You have to let me explain, Ginny. At least listen to me while I try. It's not what you think, I swear it.''

''Shhh.'' She touched her fingertips to his lips, then let them linger as his hot breath washed over them.

He was fine, she told herself. He was going to be just fine. ''I'll listen to anything you have to say, but not now, okay?''

He nodded, his color pasty now.

She kept remembering the conviction with which Marc had argued with Antonio to take him instead of her and the baby. He'd willingly put himself in this position to save her and Hannah.

And he said he loved her. Surely his actions here today said that more clearly than any words ever could.

Ginny let that certainty settle over her.

She reminded herself that she knew this man so well. Whatever else he'd done didn't seem so important now. Not when she kept remembering what it had felt like to watch him walk out that door with Antonio's gun pointed at his back. Not when she kept hearing the sound of the gun going off or the call on the radio that had told her someone was injured. Not when it had taken her what felt like forever to get to him and reassure herself that he was going to make it.

It occurred to Ginny that he understood this scene all too well, that he'd lived this very chain of events with Joe a year ago.

Joe had died in this man's arms. Joe had been like a brother to him. Marc would never betray Joe.

She looked down at Marc, lying on the ground, his eyes closed, but his chest still rising and falling in a rhythm that did much to reassure her. The blood flow from the arm had diminished greatly with the pressure and the elevation of the arm. The sirens sounded closer with every passing moment.

She couldn't bring herself to ask about Joe's cousin's condition; she just kept thinking about how hurt the whole family was going to be by what Antonio had done.

And then Ginny tried to force the whole thing from her mind, and she just held on to Marc, held on to the memory of the sound of his voice telling her he loved her.

She wasn't going to lose him now.

The hospital emergency room was zoolike. Ginny didn't think she'd ever get through, despite the police escort. They wouldn't let her anywhere near Marc's room, and soon the whole Reed family had descended on the place.

Ginny found herself having to confirm the horrible news the disbelieving relatives had already been told by the police—that Antonio had been involved with Renata Leone's killers and with Joe's death.

She made sure they all understood who had saved her and Hannah today, who'd been fighting on their side the whole time. Mama Reed wasn't ready to accept that just yet, but then, she was still in shock. She had to try to understand how one of her nephews had been indirectly responsible for her son's death.

It would take some time, a lot of time.

Ginny didn't get to see Marc until the following morning. He'd gone from surgery to recovery where he'd slept the entire night. It frightened her, being sent home for the night before she could at least see him and reassure herself that he was indeed fine.

But she was there first thing in the morning, sitting by the side of his bed, when he opened his eyes.

She had to blink back fresh tears brought on by a sense of relief that was stronger than any she'd ever known. She held his hand, let the warmth of his touch and the surprising strength of it reassure her.

Before she knew it, she was crying in earnest, her head against his chest, his hand in her hair, his lips there, too.

"Shhh," he said softly.

Ginny straightened, finally, her tears cried out. She pulled her hair back out of her eyes and took a good long look at him. He was still pale, and his eyes looked tired, his expression unreadable.

"I'm sorry," she said. "It was a long night."

"And one hell of a long day yesterday."

She nodded. "I was so worried about you."

"And I was worried about you, sweetheart. I didn't think I'd ever get to you, and then I didn't think I'd ever get Antonio and that damned gun of his out of there."

"He's going to make it," she added, in case he didn't know. "He's still critical, but the doctors say he'll pull through."

"Good. I want to hear him explain this whole thing in detail."

"Me too."

"Everything he told us yesterday fits," Marc said. "Joe must have heard something or seen something to make him suspicious of Antonio. I think he must not have had the proof he needed, otherwise he would have told someone. And when he had the proof, he would have made Antonio turn himself in.''

''I know.''

''I think that's why he was outside that apartment building, to get the proof he needed.''

''It's just so hard to believe.''

''And all these months... Ginny, when I think about you and Hannah being there in that house, about how he must have watched you and waited for some sign that Joe could have left something else behind to incriminate him... it's been driving me crazy. I don't know what I would have done if he'd hurt either one of you.''

''He didn't, thanks to you.''

''I should have figured it out,'' Marc insisted. ''Joe would have gone to hell and back to protect his family.''

Ginny knew she had some explaining of her own to do. ''I'm sorry I didn't believe you yesterday. I'm sorry I left the way I did.''

Marc didn't say anything, but he looked surprised. She knew she'd hurt him the other day.

''If I hadn't been so quick to believe Antonio, instead of you...'' She felt absolutely sick about it. ''If I hadn't gone with him, none of this would have happened.''

''Ginny, he was right. I was working for internal affairs, and we were investigating Joe. You understand that, don't you?''

She nodded.

''Then I think I'm the one who should be explaining.''

''Trust goes both ways,'' she said. ''And I know you better than to believe what he was saying.''

With effort, he managed to take a deep breath. Ginny put her hand to the side of his face, and was relieved to feel him turn in to her touch. She stroked his cheek with her thumb and let her fingers settle in his hair.

His eyelashes flickered downward, and with only the slightest urging from him, she settled her lips against his, in a lingering kiss that had both of them moaning before it ended.

Ginny sighed, then tried to smile.

Marc kissed her hand again and started to talk. "I didn't want to do it. I swear to you, when IAD came to me, it was the last thing on earth I wanted to do."

"I know. I had a lot of time to think last night, and as soon as I did, I knew there must be some explanation, because I understand how much Joe meant to you."

"He did." He nodded. "But I had all these questions about what was going on at the end, just like you did. I had to know. And IAD made it clear to me that if I didn't help them investigate Joe, they'd find someone who would. One way or another, the job was going to get done. And I knew how much it was going to hurt you and the whole family. Ginny, believe me, the last thing on earth I wanted to do was hurt you."

"I know that, too." There wasn't one shred of doubt in her mind.

"The thing that convinced me to do it was knowing you wanted the same answers, and knowing that no one else was going to work harder than I would to find the proof we needed that Joe was innocent. But the thing that tore me apart was thinking that you and I were finally going to have a chance to be together, and that when this whole investigation went public, you might hate me for what I did."

She understood perfectly. Ginny could honestly say that if someone was going to investigate her husband's death, there was no one else she'd trust more than Marc.

"Marc, I was angry and shocked, that was all. I could never hate you."

"Thank you," he said. "That means a great deal to me. Ginny, you mean the world to me. You and Hannah. I know this whole thing has been crazy, that it's all happened so fast, but I know how I feel. I don't have any doubts. I want you to marry me."

She hesitated, the moment of truth was upon them. She'd searched her heart in the time it took to get out of her house and find him. She'd gone through a million things in her mind while she wondered if she'd lost him. Her answer was clear.

"I love you, Ginny," he rushed on. "Do you think you could ever—"

She silenced him with her fingers. "I had a little talk with Hannah this morning, and it seems she'd very much like to have a dad. I don't think I could find a finer father for her than you."

"I'm afraid I want a lot more than that, sweetheart."

Ginny had one reservation left; and if they could get over that... "Marc, you know how long Joe and I tried to have a baby. You know the doctors said it was an absolute miracle I managed to carry Hannah to term."

"I know."

"Well, you have to think about this. I might not be able to give you children."

"Ginny, as far as I'm concerned, we have a child. We have Hannah."

"And that will be enough?"

"I won't deny that I'd love to have a houseful of kids, and if it happens, I'll be thrilled. If it doesn't, there are lots of children out there who need someone to love them. You and I both know that. If we want to fill up our house with children to love, we'll do it."

"Oh, Marc."

"And I hope you already know it, but I want to say it anyway—I couldn't love Hannah any more than I already do. I know she'll always be Joe's daughter, but there's no reason she can't be mine, as well. There's plenty of love in that little girl for both of us."

"Love." There was so much of it in this remarkable man.

He nodded. "Say it, Ginny. Say it today. Say it tomorrow. Say it in the church on the corner, with the whole family looking on."

Ginny smiled through her tears, all hesitation gone, as she gave him the words he wanted to hear.

"I love you, Marc. I'd be proud to be your wife."

Epilogue

Eighteen months later

He woke her with a light kiss on the lips that quickly turned into much more. Half dreaming, Ginny rolled over in the big, wide bed and pulled him to her. Her mouth opened eagerly beneath his as she welcomed him home.

Her hands ran over him, finding him in his street clothes, with his shoulder holster and his gun still in place. He must have just walked into the house and come straight into the bedroom to her.

"I missed you," she said against his lips, gasping as his hand slipped inside the delicate folds of her nightgown and found one of her breasts. She arched up against his touch, letting him know she wanted more.

"I missed you, too," he said, taking her mouth again.

And then a little rocket launched itself across the bed and jumped onto his back. "I miz 'oo, too!"

Marc smiled as he pulled away, placed his revolver o
top of the bureau, then turned to his daughter, who
twenty-two months had just learned to climb out of h
crib and was generally terrorizing their new home
scaling everything and finding her way into every encl
sure imaginable.

He tried so hard to put on that stern-daddy face for he
but it was hopeless. Hannah had him wrapped around h
little finger now, even more so than she had at fo
months. Before five seconds had passed, he was holdi
out his arms to her, and she launched herself at hi
wrapping her little arms around his neck and giving hi
a big squeeze, then a sloppy wet kiss on the cheek.

In her granny gown, with the lace and ribbons and ru
fles she liked so much, her golden curls just like h
mother's, she looked like an angel, but in this case, loo
were quite deceiving.

"Hannah, my love, what are you doing out of bed?
he said. "It's after ten."

"I miz 'oo, too," she repeated, as if that explaine
everything.

"Oh, well, I missed you, too, but you're going to be
grumpy girl in the morning if you don't get some sleep.

Hannah just grinned and squeezed him tighter.

"I'll take her back to her room," Ginny said, starti
to get up.

But Hannah wouldn't hear of that. She knew Dad
was much easier to manipulate than her mama. She clu
to him as tightly as possible and said, "Daddy read," ov
and over again.

"All right, I'll take her," Marc said.

Ginny taunted him as he picked up Hannah and walke
toward the bedroom door. "Pushover."

"You stay right there, Mrs. Dalton. When I come back, I'll show you what a pushover I am."

She heard him and Hannah chattering as they made their way down the hall, heard the negotiations going hot and heavy.

"One story."

"Two."

"One, and you don't dare climb out of this crib again until morning."

"Two."

"Hannah?"

"San'a book?"

"Santa's going to be here himself in a few days, sugar babe."

And so it went. Fifteen minutes later, he was back. With a determined grin, he closed the bedroom door behind him and locked it. Then he started unbuttoning his shirt. "Don't say it," he warned.

"Let me guess, you read three?" Ginny got to her knees and pushed his hands out of the way, so that she could undo the buttons herself.

"No, I just waited until she was asleep. It seemed like the safest thing to do, after I had her show me how she gets out of that crib. Good God, she's half monkey."

"And spoiled and stubborn." Ginny got the shirt undone and pulled it off of him.

"And gorgeous, like her mother." Marc pulled down the straps of her nightgown until it rested just above the crest of her breasts.

"She has you down cold," Ginny said. "She knows just what to do to get what she wants from you."

"Just like her mother." Marc's eyes darkened as his hands ran down the sides of her face, down her throat, down her arms, then along the curve of her breasts. Her

nipples puckered, her heartbeat quickened, and she wer
into his arms.

"What do you want, Ginny?"

That was easy. She ran her hands over his powerfull
muscled arms, then briefly over the scar that remaine
near his left shoulder, where the bullet had gone in on tha
awful night that now seemed so long ago. Her life ha
changed so much since then.

"I think Santa came early this year," she said.

"Oh?"

Ginny nodded. "I want you."

He turned all coy on her. "Oh, I don't know. I'd ha
to indulge you."

"Indulge me?" She pulled back and thought abou
ways to torment him. She let the straps of her nightgow
fall all the way down, until she was bare to the waist, an
then she brought herself closer, inch by inch, until he
breasts were nestled against his bare chest. She nipped a
his shoulder, at his neck, then slid her arms around hir
and cupped his hips, pulling him to her until he groanec

"I love you, Ginny," he said as he lowered her to th
bed.

Ginny closed her eyes and kissed him back. She wante
to remember everything about this moment. She wante
to store it away in her treasure chest of memories, the or
that was already full to the point of overflowing. At tim
like these, her happiness made her feel like the wealthie
woman on earth.

"Marc?" she said, before things got too out of hand

"Hmmm?"

"There is one more little thing I want."

"Oh?" He finally pulled back just enough to look
her.

"I want another baby."

"You do?" He suddenly turned serious.

"Yes."

"Well, you know where babies come from, don't you?"

"Yes."

"Than let's make a baby, Mrs. Dalton."

She put her hand to the side of his face, cupping his jaw, holding him just far enough away from her that she could look into his beautiful dark eyes.

"That's what I'm trying to tell you. I already got my Christmas wish."

"What?" He didn't move a muscle.

"We already made a baby."

Marc didn't so much as blink for the longest time, just stared down at her, until his eyes turned all watery and a look of pure awe came over him. He rolled off her and slid his hand down to her stomach and let it rest there for the longest time.

"A baby?"

"You know—Hannah in miniature. Before she learned to talk. Remember those days?"

"I remember."

Ginny knew he was scared, but she wasn't. "It's going to be fine," she promised him. "I know it."

Marc pressed his lips to her stomach, then turned so that his head was resting there above their baby and she could see his face. One of his hands was in her hair, caught in her curls.

"I love you," he said again.

"I love you, too."

* * * * *

As seen on TV!
Free Gift Offer

With a Free Gift proof-of-purchase from any Silhouette® book
you can receive a beautiful cubic zirconia pendant.

This gorgeous marquise-shaped stone is a genuine cubic
zirconia—accented by an 18" gold tone necklace.

(Approximate retail value $19.95)

Send for yours today...
compliments of *Silhouette*®

To receive your free gift, a cubic zirconia pendant, send us one original proof-of-
purchase, photocopies not accepted, from the back of any Silhouette Romance®,
Silhouette Desire®, Silhouette Special Edition®, Silhouette Intimate Moments®
or Silhouette Yours Truly™ title available in August, September, October, November and
December at your favorite retail outlet, together with the Free Gift Certificate, plus a
check or money order for $1.65 U.S./$2.15 CAN. (do not send cash) to cover postage and
handling, payable to Silhouette Free Gift Offer. We will send you the specified gift. Allow
6 to 8 weeks for delivery. Offer good until December 31, 1996 or while quantities last.
Offer valid in the U.S. and Canada only.

Free Gift Certificate

Name: _____

Address: _____

City: _____ State/Province: _____ Zip/Postal Code: _____

Mail this certificate, one proof-of-purchase and a check or money order for postage
and handling to: SILHOUETTE FREE GIFT OFFER 1996. In the U.S.: 3010 Walden
Avenue, P.O. Box 9077, Buffalo NY 14269-9077. In Canada: P.O. Box 613, Fort Erie,
Ontario L2Z 5X3.

FREE GIFT OFFER
084-KMD

ONE PROOF-OF-PURCHASE

To collect your fabulous FREE GIFT, a cubic zirconia pendant, you must include this
original proof-of-purchase for each gift with the properly completed Free Gift Certificate.

084-KMD

FAST CASH 4031 DRAW RULES
NO PURCHASE OR OBLIGATION NECESSARY

ifty prizes of $50 each will be awarded in random drawings to be conducted no later than 3/28/97 rom amongst all eligible responses to this prize offer received as of 2/14/97. To enter, follow directions, affix 1st-class postage and mail OR write Fast Cash 4031 on a 3" x 5" card along with your ame and address and mail that card to: Harlequin's Fast Cash 4031 Draw, P.O. Box 1395, Buffalo, IY 14240-1395 OR P.O. Box 618, Fort Erie, Ontario L2A 5X3. (Limit: one entry per outer envelope; ill entries must be sent via 1st-class mail.) Limit: one prize per household. Odds of winning are etermined by the number of eligible responses received. Offer is open only to residents of the U.S. except Puerto Rico) and Canada and is void wherever prohibited by law. All applicable laws and reglations apply. Any litigation within the province of Quebec respecting the conduct and awarding of a rize in this sweepstakes maybe submitted to the Régie des alcools, des courses et des jeux. In rder for a Canadian resident to win a prize, that person will be required to correctly answer a timemited arithmetical skill-testing question to be administered by mail. Names of winners available fter 4/28/97 by sending a self-addressed, stamped envelope to: Fast Cash 4031 Draw Winners, .O. Box 4200, Blair, NE 68009-4200.

OFFICIAL RULES
MILLION DOLLAR SWEEPSTAKES
NO PURCHASE NECESSARY TO ENTER

- To enter, follow the directions published. Method of entry may vary. For eligibility, entries must be received no later than March 31, 1998. No liability is assumed for printing errors, lost, late, non-delivered or misdirected entries.

  To determine winners, the sweepstakes numbers assigned to submitted entries will be compared against a list of randomly pre-selected prize winning numbers. In the event all prizes are not claimed via the return of prize winning numbers, random drawings will be held from among all other entries received to award unclaimed prizes.

- Prize winners will be determined no later than June 30, 1998. Selection of winning numbers and random drawings are under the supervision of D. L. Blair, Inc., an independent judging organization whose decisions are final. Limit: one prize to a family or organization. No substitution will be made for any prize, except as offered. Taxes and duties on all prizes are the sole responsibility of winners. Winners will be notified by mail. Odds of winning are determined by the number of eligible entries distributed and received.

- Sweepstakes open to residents of the U.S. (except Puerto Rico), Canada and Europe who are 18 years of age or older, except employees and immediate family members of Torstar Corp., D. L. Blair, Inc., their affiliates, subsidiaries, and all other agencies, entities, and persons connected with the use, marketing or conduct of this sweepstakes. All applicable laws and regulations apply. Sweepstakes offer void wherever prohibited by law. Any litigation within the province of Quebec respecting the conduct and awarding of a prize in this sweepstakes must be submitted to the Régie des alcools, des courses et des jeux. In order to win a prize, residents of Canada will be required to correctly answer a time-limited arithmetical skill-testing question to be administered by mail.

- Winners of major prizes (Grand through Fourth) will be obligated to sign and return an Affidavit of Eligibility and Release of Liability within 30 days of notification. In the event of non-compliance within this time period or if a prize is returned as undeliverable, D. L. Blair, Inc. may at its sole discretion award that prize to an alternate winner. By acceptance of their prize, winners consent to use of their names, photographs or other likeness for purposes of advertising, trade and promotion on behalf of Torstar Corp., its affiliates and subsidiaries, without further compensation unless prohibited by law. Torstar Corp. and D. L. Blair, Inc., their affiliates and subsidiaries are not responsible for errors in printing of sweepstakes and prizewinning numbers. In the event a duplication of a prizewinning number occurs, a random drawing will be held from among all entries received with that prizewinning number to award that prize.

SWP-S12ZD1

5. This sweepstakes is presented by Torstar Corp., its subsidiaries and affiliates in conjunctio with book, merchandise and/or product offerings. The number of prizes to be awarded an their value are as follows: Grand Prize — $1,000,000 (payable at $33,333.33 a year f 30 years); First Prize — $50,000; Second Prize — $10,000; Third Prize — $5,000; 3 Four Prizes — $1,000 each; 10 Fifth Prizes — $250 each; 1,000 Sixth Prizes — $10 each. Valu of all prizes are in U.S. currency. Prizes in each level will be presented in different creati executions, including various currencies, vehicles, merchandise and travel. Any presentati of a prize level in a currency other than U.S. currency represents an approximate equivalent the U.S. currency prize for that level, at that time. Prize winners will have the opportunity selecting any prize offered for that level; however, the actual non U.S. currency equivale prize, if offered and selected, shall be awarded at the exchange rate existing at 3:00 P.M New York time on March 31, 1998. A travel prize option, if offered and selected by winne must be completed within 12 months of selection and is subject to: traveling companion(completing and returning a Release of Liability prior to travel; and hotel and flight accor modations availability. For a current list of all prize options offered within prize levels, se a self-addressed, stamped envelope (WA residents need not affix postage) to: MILLIO DOLLAR SWEEPSTAKES Prize Options, P.O. Box 4456, Blair, NE 68009-4456, USA.

6. For a list of prize winners (available after July 31, 1998) send a separate, stampe self-addressed envelope to: MILLION DOLLAR SWEEPSTAKES Winners, P.O. Box 445 Blair, NE 68009-4459, USA.

EXTRA BONUS PRIZE DRAWING
NO PURCHASE OR OBLIGATION NECESSARY TO ENTER

7. The Extra Bonus Prize will be awarded in a random drawing to be conducted no later th 5/30/98 from among all entries received. To qualify, entries must be received by 3/31/98 a comply with published directions. Prize ($50,000) is valued in U.S. currency. Prize will presented in different creative expressions, including various currencies, vehicles, mercha dise and travel. Any presentation in a currency other than U.S. currency represents a approximate equivalent to the U.S. currency value at that time. Prize winner will have t opportunity of selecting any prize offered in any presentation of the Extra Bonus Pri Drawing; however, the actual non U.S. currency equivalent prize, if offere and selected by winner, shall be awarded at the exchange rate existing at 3:00 P.M. New Yo time on March 31, 1998. For a current list of prize options offered, send a self-addresse stamped envelope (WA residents need not affix postage) to: Extra Bonus Prize Optio P.O. Box 4462, Blair, NE 68009-4462, USA. All eligibility requirements and restrictions of MILLION DOLLAR SWEEPSTAKES apply. Odds of winning are dependent upon number eligible entries received. No substitution for prize except as offered. For the name of winn (available after 7/31/98), send a self-addressed, stamped envelope to: Extra Bonus Pri Winner, P.O. Box 4463, Blair, NE 68009-4463, USA.

SWP-S12Z

INTIMATE MOMENTS®

™ Silhouette®

COMING NEXT MONTH

#721 WILD BLOOD—Naomi Horton
Wild Hearts

Jett Kendrick was untamable, and Kathleen Patterson had the broken heart to prove it. She hadn't even been able to hold on to their baby before tragedy struck. So why, fifteen years later, was Jett looking at her with guilt—and longing—especially when his teenage boy was near?

#722 BORROWED BRIDE—Patricia Coughlin

One minute Gabrielle Flanders was wedding-bound, the next she'd been abducted from the church! Connor DeWolfe claimed she was in grave danger—that he was the only man she could trust. But Gaby didn't think her "honeymoon" was the time to find out…or was it?

#723 THE ONE WHO ALMOST GOT AWAY—Alicia Scott
The Guiness Gang

She always got her man—and Jake Guiness was no exception. The infuriating playboy was Regina O'Doul's only lead in the case of her life, so she got *close*. But somehow pretending to be lovers had led to the real thing—and to very real danger for them both.…

#724 UNBROKEN VOWS—Frances Williams

Ex-SEAL David Chandler had nothing left to give—but for Cara Merrill, he would certainly try. The gutsy beauty needed his soldiering skills to locate her ex-fiancé. But amid their dangerous jungle mission, David found himself wanting Cara all for himself.…

#725 HERO IN HIDING—Kay David

Mercy Hamilton had one rule about Mr. Right: she had to trust him. Then dark, handsome Rio Barrigan challenged her beliefs. He was all mystery—at times warm and loving, at others almost deadly. And though he broke her cardinal rule, Mercy couldn't help but believe in him—and their love.

#726 THE BABY ASSIGNMENT—Cathryn Clare
Assignment: Romance

Agent Jack Cotter knew about guns, bad guys…but babies? On that subject he knew absolutely nothing. But single-mom-on-the-run Shelby Henderson and her bouncing baby girl taught him all he needed to know about family and fatherhood. Jack only hoped they would all survive to put what he'd learned into practice.

You're About to Become a *Privileged Woman*

Reap the rewards of fabulous free gifts and benefits with proofs-of-purchase from Silhouette and Harlequin books

Pages & Privileges™

It's our way of thanking you for buying our books at your favorite retail stores.

Harlequin and Silhouette—
the most privileged readers in the world!

For more information about Harlequin and Silhouette's PAGES & PRIVILEGES program call the Pages & Privileges Benefits Desk: 1-503-794-2499

▼™ *Silhouette*®

SIM-PP2(